DIASPORIC
VIETNAMESE
ARTISTS
NETWORK

DVAN Founders

ISABELLE THUY PELAUD

and

VIET THANH NGUYEN

Also in the series:

Constellations of Eve, by Abbigail Nguyen Rosewood

Hà Nội at Midnight

STORIES

Bảo Ninh

TRANSLATED AND EDITED BY
QUAN MANH HA AND CAB TRAN

TEXAS TECH UNIVERSITY PRESS

This book is typeset in EB Garamond. The paper used in this book meets the minimum requirements of ANSI/NISO Z39.48-1992 (R1997). ♾

Design by Hannah Gaskamp
Cover design by Hannah Gaskamp

Library of Congress Cataloging-in-Publication Data

Names: Bảo Ninh, author. | Ha, Quan Manh, translator and editor. | Tran, Cab, translator and editor.
Title: Hanoi at Midnight: Stories / Bảo Ninh; translated and edited by Quan Manh Ha and Cab Tran.
Description: Lubbock, Texas: Texas Tech University Press, [2023] | Series: Diasporic Vietnamese Artists Network Series | Summary: "The first English translation of several short stories by Bao Ninh, arguably the most famous writer in Vietnam."—Provided by publisher.
Identifiers: LCCN 2022031909 (print) | LCCN 2022031910 (ebook) |
ISBN 978-1-68283-162-5 (cloth) | ISBN 978-1-68283-1-632 (ebook)
Subjects: LCSH: Bảo Ninh—Translations into English. | LCGFT: Short stories.
Classification: LCC PL4378.9.B37 H36 2022 (print) | LCC PL4378.9.B37 (ebook) |
DDC 895.9/2233—dc23/eng/20220708
LC record available at https://lccn.loc.gov/2022031909
LC ebook record available at https://lccn.loc.gov/2022031910

Printed in the United States of America
23 24 25 26 27 28 29 30 31 / 9 8 7 6 5 4 3 2 1

Texas Tech University Press
Box 41037
Lubbock, Texas 79409-1037 USA
800.832.4042
ttup@ttu.edu
www.ttupress.org

*Dâng tặng các anh em đồng đội của tôi ở trung đoàn 24, sư
đoàn 10 bộ binh,
và những người đã chiến đấu và hy sinh cho hoà bình ở
Việt Nam.*

*For my fellow soldiers of Regiment 24, Infantry Division 10,
and the people who have fought and died for peace in
Việt Nam.*

Contents

Foreword

Bảo Ninh is internationally known for his debut novel *The Sorrow of War*, the first Vietnamese novel about the American War to be translated into English, published in 1994. Like his esteemed contemporaries, such as Nguyễn Minh Châu, Nguyễn Huy Thiệp, Lê Minh Khuê, Lê Lựu, and Nguyễn Quang Thiều, Bảo Ninh has received considerable acclaim both inside Vietnam and abroad for his penetrating fiction about the war and its aftermath. *The Sorrow of War* and his short stories represent a significant contribution to the diversity and realism of Vietnamese literature since 1986, the same year that ushered in the Reform Period in Việt Nam.

Considered one of the best Vietnamese novels about the war, *The Sorrow of War* has been translated into roughly twenty languages and has received prestigious national and international awards. In the United States the novel has gained substantial attention from critics and scholars and is widely taught in college courses on literature about the Việt Nam War. Bảo Ninh's novel eloquently depicts the traumatic memory and survivor's guilt of the male protagonist, Kiên, who is unable to return to normal life after witnessing the horrendous realities of war, the indelible deaths of his fellow soldiers, and the fragility of life when juxtaposed with the atrocity of warfare. Kiên's postwar life is characterized by regret, haunting nightmares, and tragic-heroic memories of war—all of which deviate from the patriotic themes commonly found in Vietnamese literature prior to 1986. But Bảo Ninh also writes movingly about topics other than war: his observations of daily life in contemporary Việt Nam, unfulfilled promises, domestic conflicts, and romantic love, etc. The twelve short stories in this collection are among his best, with ten of them appearing in English translation for the first time.

Serendipitous encounters are a recurring motif in Bảo Ninh's short stories: some accidental and ephemeral, others lasting longer. For instance, "Giang" depicts a romantic encounter between a recruit and the eponymous heroine at a water well in a desolate mountainous area. "301" recounts two meetings: the first between an artillery tank's crew members and the daughter of a photography studio owner, and the second between the narrator and the daughter, now an older woman. The former occurs near the end of the war, and the latter during the postwar period. "The Camp of the Seven Dwarfs" relates the fortuitous encounter during a rainy night between the narrator—a postal worker—and a soldier who survives harsh realities in an environment where people have to onerously cultivate and raise livestock to supply food for soldiers on the front. Their conversations reveal the soldier's painful memories of love, nostalgia, regret, and the sorrow of human life. In "An Unnamed Star," the meeting between a team of soldiers, a decrepit old man, and his daughter evokes the odor of gunpowder, the image of a war-torn, impoverished village, and the poignant memory of the loss of one's beloved. The shared memories during these unanticipated encounters accentuate the fragility of the human condition in both wartime and its aftermath. The tragic and romantic memories resemble shards of bomb shrapnel that exacerbate the psychological wounds caused by war. In "Untamed Winds," the characters find themselves trapped in the monstrosity of war, between love and political ideology. Similarly, "Letters from the Year of the Water Buffalo" poignantly captures the blurred line between "us" and "them," between genuine camaraderie and intense antagonism. War generates coincidences, sympathy, compassion, and even suspicion in "The Secret of the River" and "Evidence."

Bảo Ninh's stories run the gamut of human emotions: nostalgia, anguish, desolation, melancholy, and hope. His stories wistfully reimagine prewar Hà Nội, its peaceful alleys and streets, its courteous residents, and the cozy atmosphere, when family members, neighbors, and friends gather around a fire or converse in a coffee shop, as in "Hà Nội at Midnight" and "Reminiscences." Juxtaposed with this tranquility and geniality are the abandoned areas and defoliated forests caused by American bombardment and use of Agent Orange, as in "An Unnamed Star" and "Farewell to a Soldier's Life." Images of polluted rivers and streams, the pungent air filled with the stench of decomposing human corpses, and the deafening roar of helicopters and bombers hovering in the gloomy sky dominate the settings of Bảo Ninh's stories. Intertwined with these horrific images are human tears shed during farewell ceremonies, when recruits are separated from their loved ones, when parents live in fear and hope at home while their children are fighting in a war in remote regions, and when soldiers bury their brethren and burden themselves with their fallen comrades' unfulfilled wishes. The mother's sorrow in "Beloved Son" becomes unspeakable; the narrator in "Letters from the Year of the Water Buffalo" struggles in his inability to deliver a letter that Duy, a soldier from the opposite side, wrote to the latter's uncle in Hà Nội. The past continues to haunt the present; the living mourn the dead; the physical war may have ended, but the internal conflict rages on.

The characters in Bảo Ninh's stories are Vietnamese soldiers from both sides (the NVA and the ARVN),[1] young women longing for a lover's return from the battlefield, forlorn and forgotten female youth-volunteers in the remote woods, and doleful parents whose

---

1   NVA: North Vietnamese Army. ARVN: Army of the Republic of Việt Nam.

children lost their lives in the war. The majority of soldiers joined the military when they were very young, energetic, and naïve. Many of them were talented, valorous, and committed to the nationalistic cause. Tragically, the monstrous war snatched away their potential, turning the young soldiers into adversaries and then corpses. Those who fortunately survived became lost after peace was restored, and their lives were unceasingly tormented by trauma, confusion, and despondency. Their restless minds and hearts prevent them from returning to a normal postwar life. However, it should be noted that these victims of war often can rely on their loved ones for empathy, support, compassion, and understanding. Their lovers and families help mitigate the veterans' losses, alleviating their agony so that they will not fall forever into hopelessness. In the preface to *Other Moons: Vietnamese Short Stories of the American War and Its Aftermath*, Bảo Ninh states, "Writing about war is writing about peace," and his stories convey his philosophy effectively and successfully. In condemning war, the stories in *Hà Nội at Midnight* also celebrate love, hope, and the possibility for reconciliation. The humanist themes in his fiction help the reader to appreciate peace as well as the cost to achieve such peace.

"Untamed Winds," arguably Bảo Ninh's best short story, depicts the tragedy of love during wartime. When he published the story in the literary magazine *Cửa Việt* in the early 1990s, it was immediately banned by the Vietnamese government. The characters in "Untamed Winds" represent two sides of the conflict: the NVA soldiers and the civilians of the former South Việt Nam. Both sides are Vietnamese but are divided by contradictory political ideologies. The central couple's escape amid gunfire illuminates the irony of war, and the story exposes human cowardice, cruelty, and selfishness. The concluding line of the story reads: "We had shot to death the two people who most embodied peace, even if peace did finally come."

Bảo Ninh's father, Hoàng Tuệ, was a professor of Vietnamese linguistics, and the author very likely inherits his father's linguistic eloquence and virtuosity. His descriptions are poetic, artistic, and meticulous. In his fiction, the reader can imagine sounds and images vividly, whether they are the roaring of a helicopter, tank, siren, monsoon downpour, flickering fire, or a character's facial expression, a storyteller's tone of voice. Although his stories are colorful and cacophonic, at times they also resemble a pastoral Chinese painting—lurking underneath the tranquility of the setting is the turmoil of the human heart and the impending fury of war.

NGUYỄN VĂN THUẤN
SCHOOL OF EDUCATION, HUẾ UNIVERSITY

Acknowledgments

First and foremost, our most sincere thanks go to Bảo Ninh for trusting us and for granting us permission to translate his short stories into English. Because we did not fight in the war and our knowledge of many military terms and weapons is limited, he kindly explained to us the words or terms that we didn't understand in his stories. It took us almost two years to complete this project for various reasons, and we appreciate the author for his patience.

We are deeply indebted to the two anonymous reviewers of this collection. Their profound knowledge of the American War in Việt Nam, NVA soldiers and ARVN soldiers, Vietnamese culture, history, and politics, and linguistic sophistication impress us greatly. They pointed out places that we had mistranslated or misinterpreted, and they offered us valuable suggestions to make our translation flow better and stay more faithful to the originals. Their meticulous reading of the manuscript was a time-consuming and onerous task, and we are grateful for their time, insights, and constructive criticism.

Special thanks to Dr. Nguyễn Văn Thuấn, Chair of Literary Studies at Huế University in Việt Nam, for writing the foreword to this collection.

We are indebted to Hubbard Savage, our copy editor, and Travis Snyder, the acquisitions editor of Texas Tech University Press. Despite his hectic schedule, Travis always replied to our emails and inquiries promptly, constantly keeping us informed of the peer-review process. This means a lot to us. We also extend our thanks to DVAN (Diasporic Vietnamese Artists Network), especially Katherina Nguyen and Isabelle Thuy Pelaud, for their encouragement and support of this project. They worked diligently with the reviewers and with us to bring *Hà Nội at Midnight* to English-speaking readers.

This collection would not have come to fruition without the gracious assistance and dedicated support of our friends. Joseph Babcock came up with the idea for this project. Nguyễn Thị Minh Hạnh and Võ Thị Lệ Thủy found and scanned some stories that we couldn't find online. Paul Christiansen, Võ Hương Quỳnh, and Nguyễn Phan Quế Mai continuously offered us encouragement. Tạ Duy Anh and Dạ Ngân clarified some of the terms related to the war that we didn't quite grasp. We thank all of them for their kindness and friendship.

Finally, our deepest gratitude is expressed to our parents, Đinh Thị Hải, Noel Harold Kaylor, Ho Tran, and Thuy Tran, for their love, inspiration, and sacrifice to ensure us the best life possible. Also, many thanks to Lindsay Tran for her patience and devotion during the course of this project.

A Note on the Translation

Bảo Ninh has published about twenty-five short stories related to the war, and several have been translated into English: "Wandering Souls" in *The Other Side of Heaven: Post-War Fiction by Vietnamese and American Writers* (1995), "Savage Winds" in the Britain-based literary magazine *Granta* (1995), "A Marker on the Side of the Boat" in *Night, Again: Contemporary Fiction from Vietnam* (1996), "The River's Mystery" in *Love After War: Contemporary Fiction from Vietnam* (2003), and "White Clouds Flying" in *Other Moons: Vietnamese Short Stories about the American War and Its Aftermath* (2020). For this present collection, two stories have been re-translated per Bảo Ninh's request: "The Secret of the River" and "Untamed Winds."

Translating a work of fiction from one language to another is no easy task. There might be an expectation that the final result—the translated version of the work—retain as much of the original's language as possible. Ideally, any reader from any language would come away with the exact same story in their native tongue. This, of course, is impossible. Language is slippery, ever evolving, and what might make complete sense to one group of people might sound nonsensical to another. In our translation of *Hà Nội at Midnight*, we decided early on that we would try our best to preserve Bảo Ninh's poetic voice, his sense of humor, his idiosyncratic use of first-person narration, his fragmentary style of storytelling, while at the same time making his stories as accessible to the widest English-speaking audience as possible.

We chose to approach this project holistically, focusing our efforts less on the word-for-word literal translation and more on Bảo Ninh's *voice*. Not only must careful attention be paid to syntax and word choice, but there is figurative and metaphorical language to worry about, idiomatic and proverbial usage, tone, and the simple fact that certain words, phrases, and ideas will remain untranslatable. Taken together, the writer's *voice* is perhaps the least understood and yet most recognizable feature of any writer's work. Our decisions along the way reflect this line of thinking.

We kept Bảo Ninh's fragmentary style and blended use of first-person and third-person omniscient because this kind of unconventional storytelling is a hallmark of his prose. In more mainstream stories written in English, normally the point of view is clearly indicated, whether it is first-person, third-person omniscient, or third-person limited. For a variety of historic and linguistic reasons, this is not the case in Vietnamese fiction. Perspectives often shift, and details are presented from viewpoints of characters who may not logically be privy to others' thoughts and feelings. Bảo Ninh's decision to dispel with rigid point-of-view distinctions is most apparent in his two longest stories, "Untamed Winds" and "Hà Nội at Midnight." In the first—perhaps the author's most narratively complex story—the "I" narrator does not appear until much later, throwing doubt on how exactly the "I" narrator can recall in striking detail not only the events leading up to the point he inserts himself into the story, but also the fact that he has access to the innermost thoughts of other characters at all. In "Hà Nội at Midnight," what starts out in the first person shifts to something more akin to third for much of the middle, until a reversal when the narrative sleight-of-hand becomes evident and integral to the story's big reveal: that the narrator, in fact, is one of the children living at the house all along. In this way, Bảo Ninh's stylistic—and some would say problematic—use of point of view is unique among his literary peers in Việt Nam. In our translation, we have done our best to preserve this incongruity while at the same time making it less confusing for readers to follow.

To maintain consistency across the translation, we added diacritical marks to proper names and places as they would appear in the original to Vietnamese readers. With the author's express permission, we changed the names of several characters to avoid further confusion, as some characters who appear in different stories share identical names, and sometimes within the same story even though they are clearly not the same people. We do not believe this editorial change adversely affects the narratives. In the process of our translation, we trimmed down a few areas without distorting the overall shape of the story and reworded a few awkward phrases for the sake of clarity, so that events in the stories unfold in a more natural way without sacrificing any of Bảo Ninh's narrative power.

Balancing the rhythm of Bảo Ninh's descriptive prose and the Vietnamese tendency to use idiomatic and proverbial language in storytelling while staying faithful to the original was a difficult but not impossible task. Vietnamese readers will understand many of the implied messages he makes throughout his stories, but due to cultural differences, English readers might not. We gave context or an English equivalent to the more idiomatic passages and proverbs in the translation. One example is in the title "Farewell to a Soldier's Life." In the original Vietnamese, the literal translation is "Hands Washed, Sword Put Away." The latter may sound more poetic to English readers, but without any context to the Vietnamese, the title can be misleading or misunderstood entirely. As another example, a sunrise climbing the low, eastern hills in "Untamed Winds" is described as "wet" in the original, but instead we used "yolk-like," which is closer to what the author is trying to get across to his readers in Vietnamese. In keeping with the poetic nature of Vietnamese prose, we sought a translation that we believe best preserves the original's rhythm and musicality.

Although they are works of fiction, these collected stories are rooted in history. As in his first novel, *The Sorrow of War*, many of Bảo Ninh's most important themes can be found here: war and its repercussions on the human psyche, how memory informs trauma and vice versa, and ordinary people trying to make their way through a world of incredible suffering. At times, *Hà Nội at Midnight* can be overtly militaristic and political. Bảo Ninh's stories do not gloss over details about aircraft or weaponry used during the war, giving his narratives an authentic viewpoint through the eyes of their protagonists. His obsession with numbers, exact dates, the caliber of different guns, and the placement of artillery as well as locations of battlefields, the names of different military campaigns, troop movements, even the branded items carried in a soldier's rucksack all point to a writer whose work is inseparable from his own past and his memory of it. Though the more political inclinations of his characters are expressed freely and unambiguously, their politics do not define them as individuals; rather, they remain living, breathing people on the page with their own desires, goals, and beliefs. As in real life, these traits can appear contradictory on the surface. Look closer and one can see that wars waged on the battlefield are mirrored by wars waged within each character's psyche. If there is anything that Bảo Ninh's characters in these stories share, it is that the war has not left anyone unscathed, whether soldier or civilian, man or woman—not even innocent children are spared. Only by taking the story collection as a whole do we see how these contradictions interrogate and expose the raw truth of war.

But the stories in *Hà Nội at Midnight* are also stories about people in unguarded, private moments of heartbreak and revelation: a mother's final letter to her son that will never be read, two young people in love sharing a bike ride down an empty road in a remote area at dusk, a father and son sitting in a dilapidated coffee shop on the eve of the son's enlistment, an old railroad signalman with dementia waiting for a train that will never come, two young lovers with their own hopes and dreams for the future shattered in a hail of bullets. The stories collected here, many in English for the first time, are universal to the human experience, across generations and cultures, in ways both profound and ordinary, no matter the language.

QUAN MANH HA AND CAB TRAN

Hà Nội at Midnight

Farewell to a Soldier's Life

N ow, as I look back on the final days of my life as a soldier, my heart is laden with sorrow and longing. From my euphoric peak on the day of liberation to this very afternoon, the peaceful days and nights since have passed by slowly, even if our lives remain short. When I returned from the battlefield, my parents were not yet retired, but now they are in their seventies. My siblings have scattered and live elsewhere; they are also getting old. After Tết[2] this year, my son will be the same age I was when I joined the military. My wife, known for her youthfulness, no longer looks that way. The misfortunes she has endured have taken their toll. I threw myself into my work, took up all kinds of odd jobs, and finally became a writer. But I don't consider myself a good writer because I don't write a lot, and I've never had a high opinion of my work. Now I feel more alone and diminished than ever. Life and time have a way of drowning me.

I wish I had a choice to do it all over again, but given the opportunity, where would I even start? The past will always be veiled in fog. The

---

2   Vietnamese Lunar New Year.

world has changed a lot since then, and I've lost my bearings completely, along with those youthful and heroic years I spent during the war. What I remember of the long war has faded. Even the material reminders of my military life have disappeared, one after another: my rucksack, my hammock, my Souzhou uniforms, including my molded rubber sandals and green duckweed hat, the book that recorded my time in the service, the official documents detailing my injuries, and all of my personal letters and diaries. It's not that I've somehow lost them but rather that the person I once was, that soldier, no longer exists.

My fellow comrades lead their own lives now. We haven't seen each other in years, so we tend to forget. In an earlier time, you didn't have to be my friend or in the same unit, but if you were someone who fought in Front K, at Chum Field, or at the ancient citadel in Quảng Trị, then I would treat you kindly. However, I now find it difficult to become close to anyone and despise living in this indifferent city. In fact, I sometimes even forget that the head of the HR office of my company used to be the commander of the T54 tank that paved the way for our shock platoon to get through Lăng Cha Cả and attack the Tân Sơn Nhất Airport. At one time, living side by side, we survived amid bomb explosions, but nowadays we don't even say hello or acknowledge each other, as though everything we've been through together never happened.

Twenty years after the war ended, I took a flight to revisit Sài Gòn. When I disembarked from the airplane and stepped onto the asphalt runway, I felt something very strange foment inside me, repressed emotions from long ago stirring awake as though for the first time. That afternoon, a dark cloud crossed in front of the sun and cast a long shadow across the tarmac. Suddenly, my memory of the airport on the final day of April 1975 rushed back to me. But I knew it was just a fleeting illusion. What I actually heard was the roar of a Boeing passenger jet accelerating before takeoff, not the deafening pandemonium of a heated firefight. The airport was expansive, immaculate, and shiny. I recognized the air traffic control tower, which was the only thing left standing from the war, but the flag that had the words "Victory Bound" put up by Division 10 that I had seen flapping in the wind back then on the roof of the tower was gone. I looked around. Where was the sign to the MACV camp?[3] Where was the Davis Camp,[4] the place where Regiment 24 ended the war? At the Davis Camp our beloved regiment commander, Vũ Tài, carrying a pistol in his hand, had jumped down, along with my squadmates, from their tank and were surrounded and warmly greeted as heroes by a huge crowd. The tears we shed in that moment came out unexpectedly and bitterly, stinging our eyes, but they were tears of triumph nevertheless.

•

Those radiant days of victory are long over. We were assigned new tasks afterward. One squad was urgently sent to the border to deal with Pol Pot. Another squad moved to a newly liberated region to unearth mines, fill in bomb craters, and encourage civilians to complete their civic duties. I had to return to the Central Highlands to collect the remains of my fallen fellow soldiers. Unfortunately, I contracted an acute case of malaria while working on a mission in the Đông Sa Thầy jungle. I was flown to Sài Gòn by helicopter and treated at a military hospital. After my recovery, I didn't return to my unit. Instead, I was transferred to a rehabilitation center and remained there with nothing to do except wait for the day when I could be formally discharged.

During the war, the rehabilitation center had been an ARVN training school for the staff of the pacification campaign.[5] Its location

---

3   US Military Assistance Command.

4   Davis Camp used to be a unit of the US Air Force located southwest of the Tân Sơn Nhất Airport.

5   "To clear the Viet Cong from the areas they controlled and from contested villages, the United States relied on the strategy of pacification. . . . Once a hamlet or village was taken over, South Vietnamese government officials moved

near a big river turned it into an island in the rainy seasons. Where there was flooding, the water ran through barbed wire and swamped our quarters at night, bringing in filthy flotsam and jetsam that the defeated army had left behind. The water level was extremely high that year. A rain during peacetime is no different from one during times of war—it lasts forever. That year, our radiant days were replaced by the melancholy of autumnal sunsets. Water was everywhere; it rained day and night. All the vegetables we planted rotted away, leaving behind only water spinach. Our volleyball court was steeped in mud. Rain fell on the tin roofs. During lighter rainfall it sounded like insects chirping, and during heavier downpours the noise was deafening. The air was so moist that it filled our room, our clothes, and made us lethargic.

We could go nowhere because of the flooding, so we just stayed in the rehabilitation center. We played cards and chess. We chatted among ourselves and listened to music and poetry on the radio, but nothing could alleviate the boredom the rain had caused us. The humid weather and damp air made us sick and we turned pale as a result. Headaches and runny noses became common. Once, half of us fell ill and were forced to eat porridge. We became dependent on the southerners' traditional treatments of these symptoms: rubbing Nhị Thiên Đường medicated oil on our skin, massaging our foreheads and temples, and cupping our backs.

Every night near my bed, Khương, while asleep and dreaming, would grind his teeth and moan. Indistinguishable words would escape his throat. During the day, he acted as if everything was normal. He was a pleasant person to be around. He was both easygoing and sociable, not one of those people who carried around emotional

---

in to solidify control. Militia and self-defense forces were set up to provide security. Then the government would try to win hearts and minds by building schools and clinics, and begin a process of economic development leading to modernization." (Mai Elliott, "The Terrible Violence of 'Pacification,'" *New York Times*, January 18, 2018, https://www.nytimes.com/2018/01/18/opinion/violence-pacification-vietnam-war.html.)

baggage. However, usually around midnight, he would have terrible nightmares. Khương said that when he was fighting in the war, he didn't experience anything like this in his sleep. But he started to have nightmares after the country was reunified, and only after he was sent to the rehabilitation center.

The medicine he took didn't help; the pain in his sleep was not physical but psychological. Fast asleep, Khương would dream about his injury. He had been the notable scout commander of Front B3 and assigned to the battlefield during the first dry season when American infantry fought the war in the Central Highlands. He was wounded several times, dislocated some bones, and lost a lot of blood, but none of the injuries defeated him. He was able to return to his scout unit despite his severe wounds. It seemed that his battlefield struggles had strengthened him and given him the courage to endure his pain. Now, asleep, Khương would experience again all the trauma that he suffered before. The doctor said there was nothing to worry about; the nightmares coming from his unconscious mind could be mitigated, although nobody knew exactly how.

When we are awake, we can try to repress and forget, but asleep, how do we control our dreams? Not only Khương but everyone in our room at the rehabilitation center had nightmares caused by the war. For instance, Tú always revisited his encounter with a CBU bomb that was dropped in a rubber tree forest at Xuân Lộc. The trench collapsed, and as Tú was suffocating, he had the sensation of being buried alive. As for myself, I dreamed about toxic rainfall and the old forests in Ngọc Bơ Biêng being bombed by the Americans and turned into massive piles of dry wood. Back then, for several months, the sky in Ngọc Bơ Biêng was buzzing with C-123 planes slowly spraying a chemical liquid onto the green forests. We didn't know back then what the Americans were doing. Nobody knew what horrible thing was happening.

In those days, no one paid attention to the roar of aircraft above. The forest where our company spent the night wasn't dense, but it was located in a valley surrounded by high mountains so it wasn't carpet-bombed. It was our instincts that forced us from our hammocks. I remember how my face felt somewhat numb and wet. Droplets of stinging water landed on my eyelashes. I rubbed my face and eyes with my hands, yawned, sat up, and dolefully got off my hammock. I felt unusually exhausted. The sound of the aircraft was gone, but I could still sense its rumbling in the distance.

Fog cloaked the forest, or what I thought was fog. Or maybe it was smoke, some sort of viscous and wet smoke. Fallen leaves then landed on the damp netting of our hammocks. Our clothing and our bodies absorbed the dampness, which troubled us. We started to feel sluggish and weak. I smelled my hands, now covered with tiny droplets of water, but sensed nothing unusual. But didn't the air have some kind of burning smell? I looked up. The entire forest was shedding its leaves. There was no wind, no trees rustling, yet leaves were falling as though an earthquake had shaken them loose. First leaves, then flowers, crops, and saplings fell down as though a raging tempest had passed through. Foliage in every shape and size shriveled and turned a dark brown. The grass below us also was dying and changing color. In the war, I had seen much worse, more horrifying things than this, but what haunted me for the rest of my life was how the Americans, during that month, had destroyed our land with Agent Orange.

•

On the first day of May 1975, when I was still at the Tân Sơn Nhất Airport, I hurriedly sent a letter to Hà Nội informing my family that I was alive. As if it were still during wartime, I didn't receive their reply until October, around the time I was getting discharged. I also accepted mail that weighed about three pounds that my mother sent me. Incredulously, when I opened the parcel, I noticed that it was postmarked from the summer of 1973. The entire rehabilitation center looked at my package, which was shipped during the war and reached me during a time of peace. My mother had wrapped it thoughtfully, twice in thick plastic, and added an extra layer of cement-bag paper. Her letter and the parcel had traveled thousands of miles in the dry season through the fiery Trường Sơn Mountains. They had been soaked deep in mud and rain before reaching me. I couldn't read my mother's letter—the words were too faint. The candy and cookies were inedible, the cigarettes worthless. The other items—things like sewing kits and Tiger Balm—would still be useful, had the war continued.

Once, during the war, at the end of the rainy season, the corpse of a military mailman was carried by a flood from the top of the mountain down into the Pô Cô River. Then his body became lodged in a reed bed near where my unit was stationed. His corpse was covered with deep gouges caused by artillery shells. He had been dead for several days and his body had been in the water for so long that it had decomposed. Fish had eaten his flesh. He might have been shot and killed by a helicopter while trying to cross a creek upstream. A bag made from parachute canvas was still attached to his back, although it was full of holes caused by bullets. Stuffed inside the bag was mail, wet and stained with ink and blood. Water had washed away the names and addresses on the envelopes, except for the red postmarks from the North. We buried the unnamed mailman and the letters together. From then on, I stopped sending letters to my family and stopped looking forward to receiving letters and news from home. I felt that letters written to soldiers contained more bad news than good anyway, whether during war or in times of peace.

When I received my mother's package, Quang also received a letter. Although Quang wrote often, he, like me, just now got a response, and it contained bad news: his wife had been cheating on him. She had had an affair with a sailor, gotten herself pregnant and, as a result, had to flee the village and vanish with the sailor to the South just after the country was unified. Quang was calm when he got the news because he could sympathize with her situation. "After our wedding we lived as a married couple for only a week," he said, "then I had to go to the South. She had to wait for me for ten years, so of course I understand that there's a breaking point. Anyway, my house is located along a busy riverfront, so she was destined to leave me."

What Quang said didn't reflect how I truly felt. Later that night, Quang dreamed about his unfaithful wife, muttered her name in his congested voice, and mumbled something unintelligible. Quang and his wife had no children, but half of the contents of his rucksack were toys, and the rest were gifts for his wife. Now and then, we saw him unpack and repack fabric, yarn, silk underwear with black frills, small bottles of perfume, beads, necklaces, and bracelets. He didn't drink or smoke, so he was able to save a decent amount of money. Every day, he wrote his wife a long letter but never mailed it. He kept his letters bundled, and in the afternoon before he said goodbye to us and left for his hometown, he took the pile of letters to the riverbank and read all of them. Afterward, he tore the letters into pieces and threw them into the river. Tú and I happened to be fishing nearby, and he remarked, "Must be love letters for carp."

It was sunny and clear that afternoon, so Tú and I didn't play cards but had decided to go fishing instead. The sun loomed in the afternoon sky; in the wind, golden waves glittered and rolled from east to west. The horizon seemed immense, as an untroubled life emerged from the clear sunset. I heard the river's unhurried breath and saw the dark clouds dissipate overhead. On the far side of the river, the city appeared bright in the afternoon's sunbeams. A mist gathering over the river slowly turned toward the setting sun. Along the road across from a nearby empty field, trucks moved as though they were skating on fog.

Tú and I didn't catch any fish that day, so we returned to the rehabilitation center in time for dinner. When we saw skinny Quang with his slightly hunched back, Tú joked, "You'll be returning back to the North tomorrow, Quang, so why the long face?"

"I don't plan on going back to my hometown," he said. "I need to find my wife first. I'll look everywhere if I have to. I don't care how long it takes. It's the dry season now, so I hope that makes searching for her a little easier."

"Right, the dry season . . ." I said.

I knew the situation should improve for everybody now that it was the dry season—that was my hope but also the belief of many who had spent time on the battlefield. Rainy seasons tended to be long and tedious, but they did end eventually. The sun would come out and turn the world idyllic again, rekindling the hopes any of us held for the future.

It was the first time while sharing a room with Quang at the rehabilitation center that I didn't see him act despondent. That evening, we threw a small going-away party for him. He got very drunk and animated.

"I've been thinking about this a lot," Quang said. "After I find my wife, we'll resettle in the South and not go back up North. In the South, there're lots of wide-open spaces and big, winding rivers. We won't worry about how to make a living there. Anyway, I prefer the southerners' spirit and way of life. They're not as conservative and set in their old ways. And they're very generous . . . "

Quang left the rehabilitation center the next day. He didn't take the bus, but walked, carrying his rucksack on his back. Instead of heading in the direction of the city, or toward the North, he walked slowly along the river, determined to begin his solitary journey to find his wife and a new home.

Khương, and then Tú, left the center a few days later as well. The facility emptied out, and when we said our goodbyes, we mentioned nothing about meeting up in the future. We looked at each other, exchanged firm handshakes, and doled out words of encouragement. We were fellow soldiers who aspired to the same goals. But now, although our lives took us in different directions, our hearts would remain unchanged, and the camaraderie of our time spent together could never be forgotten.

A few days before I left the rehabilitation center, I met Loan by accident. She had been my classmate and we lived in the same town. Loan, a second lieutenant medic, wore a uniform and carried a short gun and a satchel. She was pale and skinny, with short-cropped hair. I saw her getting out of a car with a delegation led by a general and I called out, "Loan, baby-faced Loan!" She was surprised when she recognized me, trembled, and lost her balance momentarily. Color drained from her face as she forced a smile. While the general was visiting the camp, I invited her into my barracks room, which looked deserted and gloomy, since I was the only one living there now. I opened all the windows in a hurry, then neatly stacked the sleeping mats and blankets in a corner. I asked her to take a seat at the foot of a bed. I put some sweets on the table. We talked for an hour by an open window and gazed out at the garden. The afternoon breeze carried a pleasant scent. Leaves rustled outside. She said it had been years since someone had called her by her nickname, "baby-faced Loan," which had annoyed her deeply in high school. But now, hearing the moniker again made her want to cry. She said it was unlikely any of the "baby-ness" she had once possessed still remained. She wondered if any of the other male classmates who had teased her with this name were still alive. For an hour, we sat in the afternoon sunlight and shared memories of our past like old lovers. We talked about our hometown, Bưởi High School, our Class 10C, and our classmates, who all at one point had huddled together in combat trenches and many of whom had died in the war.

Loan recounted that after the Tết holiday of 1973, the Year of the Water Buffalo, she attended a class reunion at the house of our former teacher. There was only one male attendee, Khoa, who had just graduated in the Soviet Union with a degree in literature. The atmosphere of the reunion was poignant because half of the class was missing, since they either had died in the war or were presumed dead—nobody had heard anything about them. Likewise, the other classes in our school and town received either sad news or no news at all about their male classmates. When Loan and I met, I was the only one she had encountered since the day all the men enlisted in the war.

Now that I think about it, besides me, Loan did meet another man, named Hải, who lived in the same town. It was at a military treatment facility on the Thượng Đức Front, in the rainy season of 1974. Hải had been a local policeman before he enlisted, and he recognized Loan immediately when he saw her, but Loan didn't know Hải from before, and she wouldn't have recognized him anyway because he was severely disfigured. He had scars on his face and his body was misshapen. The pain he experienced, however, caused his eyes to remain wide open. After his surgery, Hải suffered severely even while his mind remained sharp. During treatment in the underground tunnels, Loan remained by Hải's side and together they waited for the sun to rise. It had rained heavily and they could hear the sound of artillery fire coming from beyond the trenches. Hải told Loan to lie down next to him and to put her arm under his head so that he had something for his head to rest on. Hải died in the early morning, but his body remained warm until Loan moved her arm away from his corpse.

I gently held Loan's hands. The afternoon sun was peaceful. While we were overwhelmed by memories of sorrow and friendship, the driver honked to signal for Loan to come out and join the delegation for the return trip. The late afternoon sunlight poured into the window and filled the room with crimson hues. In the garden, trees and leaves quivered in the strong wind. I gripped her hands more firmly.

"Please don't do that," Loan whispered, withdrawing her hands from mine. "But I'm glad I met you here. It's a gorgeous afternoon."

Silently, we fell into each other. After a tepid kiss we pulled away. Loan left me alone and fled the room. Two days later, I was discharged. A final send-off to my soldierly life.

I left early in the morning when the ground was still damp under my feet. I saw rows of empty buildings leading from the gate to the rehabilitation center and heard the familiar iron gong—the husk of a defused bomb—signaling the routine of our past days. Its echoing disturbed the tranquility of the entire riverbank.

I pulled down my hat to shield my eyes from the sun and walked solemnly. The dry season was here, but it seemed as though it had arrived a long time ago. The suburbs were covered in dust. Mangled tanks were scattered along the roadways and even inside cemetery grounds. The tin roofs of factories and warehouses had collapsed in on themselves. Advertisement billboards were full of holes caused by gunfire. Church steeples, walls, and brick gates had fallen into ruin, but the markets and river ports were showing activity and signs of life again. The liberated South might be in ruins, but there was hope that conditions would improve in the future. Although it might take years for us to enjoy our new, brighter future, most of us—the veterans of the Victory Division—could rest at ease knowing that we would be alive to witness it.

No matter how young we were then, by shouldering the memories of war that seemed heavy as a thousand-year burden, we felt as though we had lived through the most profound years of our lives. Later in life, we would remind ourselves that whatever misfortunes we encountered were nothing compared to those we experienced as soldiers. We were a young generation who became men in the trenches and on the battlefields, and this was what gave our lives meaning. And if we were to find happiness, we would always remember that no amount of happiness could overshadow our time spent together in the war. The war, and our friendship, was what made us who we are.

Beloved Son

That trunk, which Tân hadn't minded carrying with him all the way from Hà Nội, was abandoned in a corner and mostly forgotten. But now, a year has passed, and his maid cleans out the storage room in the basement. She drags the trunk into the front yard hoping she can throw it out.

"It looks like a coffin," Tân's eldest daughter jokes.

"That thing doesn't belong in our home," Tân's wife adds.

The truth of it is that he doesn't have any good reason to keep the trunk, but he has sentimental feelings for it and thinks he should save at least one thing as a memento of his mother. It matters little since she has already passed away, but the house where his parents once lived had been sold. He also knows it wouldn't have been right to keep their house in shambles. Tân's older sister warned him about hoarding, and he, of course, has no intention of becoming a hoarder. Tân's older brother inherited the TV and his sister got the refrigerator. As for Tân, he reluctantly chose the trunk sitting next to his mother's bed. He hailed a taxi afterward for the airport. It was a shabby-looking trunk, neither too heavy nor ornate, but he remembered it from high school when he was a student during an evacuation.

Now Tân tells the maid to dust off the trunk; he would find a way to open it himself. The key is lost, but the lid pries open easily. A slight odor—that of mothballs—escapes into the air. He finds nothing valuable inside, only discolored letters and other ephemera like his and his siblings' school records, report cards, and award certificates. Also inside is a small album containing stamp-sized photos and a few letters that Tân's brother had sent from the Soviet Union, his sister's correspondence from East Germany, and even letters from Tân himself when he was in Czechoslovakia. At the bottom of the trunk, he discovers a thick and somewhat hefty package carefully wrapped in newspaper. He thinks it's most likely another bundle of letters, or a book containing the family's subsidized ration cards, or possibly even a stack of coupons for clothing material and food.

Tân's sister often complained, "Mom's so set in her old ways. Everybody else gets rid of junk that reminds them of how hard life used to be, but Mom keeps everything." One look at their mother's apartment would reveal that all the furniture was as old as its owner, left intact and unchanged over the years. Her sons and daughter had begged her to move in with them in their villas, but she had refused to relocate anywhere outside her building. She was old and lived alone, and she disliked the idea of hiring a live-in maid.

"We're afraid about her not wanting to move," Tân's sister once said to him. "What should we do? We've already asked her if there's anything that could make her life easier and she just shakes her head and says no. We're not better or worse off than other families. Am I right? Me, you, our brother—we're all successful now, and so are her son-in-law and daughters-in-law. Her grandchildren are doing fine and are well-behaved. Their future looks promising. So, I have no idea why Mom is so stubborn about wanting to live by herself. What do you think is her problem?"

Neither Tân nor his sister can remember how their mother had lived back then, whether grief or happiness was the prevailing condition of her life. But he knows one thing: something changed in her old age. When she was still alive, he had no concerns for her health. Her eyesight was still good and she was sprightly enough to move around on her own. Her mind remained sharp. She used to assure Tân of her good health whenever he visited her from Sài Gòn. The family was also in good standing: Tân, along with his brother and sister, had all relocated to the South, but even from far away they showed their mother deference and love. During the subsidy period, all three children lived better than most they knew, and now they are faring extremely well. As a result, they always provided their mother with whatever she needed and took good care of her. But that didn't explain her overall dissatisfaction with life. Worse, she looked more dispirited every year and none of her children knew why.

•

At the bottom of the trunk are letters wrapped in old newspaper written by Tân's mother to his younger brother. All the letters are addressed to Nghĩa and had been sent to a single post office number, though all were returned to the sender. Not one of them had been opened.

Tân sits quietly, trying to understand his odd predicament. He's in no hurry to open the first letter. The truth of it is he did have a younger brother. One time, while filling out some background forms, Tân even forgot to list Nghĩa as a family member. It probably slipped the minds of his siblings too. They often said, "The three of us," and in their minds, gradually, the image of their youngest sibling faded over time without much notice, finally disappearing altogether. When they were kids, they all had their photographs taken, but by the time they reached adolescence there remained almost no visual records. Tân keeps around a photo of himself taken during Tết when he was seventeen. Nghĩa could have looked the same as him back then. In the discolored photo, Tân stands next to a leafless catappa tree in front of a dilapidated apartment. Scattered across the grounds are used-up firecrackers. He is wearing a cotton jacket and a PUL fabric scarf in the photo. He looks gloomy, pensive, as he tries to crack a smile in front of the camera. In the photo, his expression is one that reveals an even earlier memory of boyhood, long forgotten, bubbling to the surface. Now, Tân can remember nothing about his life before reaching seventeen, when he left the country to study abroad.

What happened in those childhood years before then? War, evacuation, horror. People were terrified by constant bombings, artillery fire, and having to live hand to mouth. But compared to other families in the building, Tân's family was better off financially. That didn't matter much, however, because the situation in their tenement, even for a state official's family, typically devolved into conflicts between neighbors. The monotony, coupled with the misery of living under such dire conditions, was not worth remembering. Tân only recalls having little say in the matter, except that he had to work extremely hard to get the credit he deserved, so that after finishing the tenth grade he could go study abroad like his brother and sister.

After studying in Czechoslovakia for a year, Tân received a letter from his mother informing him of Nghĩa's enlistment. Nghĩa had received his matriculation letter from the University of Technology before the enlistment letter, but he refused to listen to his parents' advice. That was his temperament, the way he had always been. What Tân can remember is that, since childhood, his youngest brother had always been an impulsive and mischievous child. Unlike his other siblings, Nghĩa had often gone against their father's wishes. Their stoic father was a man defined by his equanimity, so when he did lash out, they knew that Nghĩa was responsible.

In her letter to Tân, his mother wrote that Nghĩa's refusal to go to college had created friction between him and his father—right up until the day Nghĩa left to join the military. His mother, of course, felt sorry for her youngest son, whose path in life was much more complicated than that of his siblings. She gave Tân the post office number Nghĩa used, urging him to write to his younger brother to cheer him up. She said she had visited Nghĩa at the training camp for new conscripts in Bãi Nai, Hòa Bình Province, and that the hardships he experienced there broke her heart. Back then, Tân had read the letter but felt indifferent to his brother's plight. Now, reading his mother's letter to Nghĩa makes him realize again how much his mother had loved her youngest child.

People say that when living in the woods, you should never take a nap, even if you're exhausted, because you might contract malaria while sleeping. That would be detrimental to your health, and I live too far away to take care of you. I often worry about your risk-taking attitude toward life. Dear son, when you hear sirens, even if you don't see the enemy planes overhead, you must find a bomb shelter immediately. There's no shame in avoiding stampeding elephants.[6] If you love me and your Dad, then you must take good care of yourself.

I've wrapped these gifts in two different colors so that you can distinguish them easily. The blue package has candy, cookies, and cigarettes for you to share with your comrades and commanders. I hope you smoke less. I've heard that where you're stationed, the locals distill their own liquor, and that worries me. Drinking and smoking will ruin your life. In the red package, there are sewing kits, firestones, batteries, and hairpins. You should guard these important items with your life. They are difficult to find even in Hà Nội, and are very valuable in places like Military Region 4 and Laos.[7] They might make what you carry a little heavier, but please keep them close to you. In case you become sick, come down with the flu, or even worse, contract malaria, you can trade those things for healthy food that will nourish your body and speed up your recovery. The mothers in our neighborhood whose sons joined the military gave me these suggestions.

---

6   A Vietnamese proverb that means it is not cowardly to be cautious.
7   Military Region 4 includes these provinces in north-central Việt Nam: Thanh Hoá, Nghệ An, Hà Tĩnh, Quảng Bình, Quảng Trị, and Thừa Thiên Huế.

Tân doesn't know if those gifts ever reached Nghĩa, because it's obvious that all the letters displayed before him now were sent to Lương Sơn, after Nghĩa's unit had left the area. They had all been returned, but their mother, full of hope, remained steadfast and kept sending letters to an abandoned address. The initial ones are short, as if she wrote them in a hurry. In those first letters, she urged Nghĩa to write home and inform his parents of his new address, where he was currently stationed, and how he was holding up. As the war dragged on and time went by, her letters became longer and more distressful. Every letter she mailed out was eventually returned to her. Her later correspondence read like a diary, as though she were writing to herself. She wrote in a neat, easy-to-read script, although by this time the ink had long faded. Word after word concealed her despair. She once said she had dreamed of Nghĩa, but before she was able to call out his name, trying her best to dwell in the dream in her dark room, the wailing sirens outside woke her.

Unlike his mother, Tân's father never saw his youngest son in his dreams, but he sometimes thought he saw Nghĩa in the streets downtown, according to what Tân's mother told him. One evening, his father brought home a soldier around Nghĩa's age he had just met at Hàng Cỏ train station. When he spied the soldier milling in the crowd in front of the station, his father, who was sitting in a trolley at the time, hurriedly motioned for the driver to stop. His father got off the trolley and, pushing his way through the crowd, approached the soldier. Then he wept, "Nghĩa, Nghĩa . . ." He was always mistaking someone for his youngest son. From a short distance, any soldier could look like Nghĩa, but as he got closer, none turned out to be his son. That day, Tân's mother used all of her monthly food coupons to prepare an extraordinary feast for the soldier. His father invited the soldier to stay the night and saw him off in the morning at Kim Mã bus station. He even got in line to buy a bus ticket for the young man and escorted him to his seat on the bus. The soldier later lost his hand to a bullet and also went blind. On another occasion, Tân's father thought he saw Nghĩa among a group of intelligence officers in a photo in the periodical *Military*; his mother wanted to believe it was true, too. There were rumors that it was less dangerous to work in intelligence than it was to be an infantryman. But the following morning, his father looked at the photo again, shook his head, and said, "No, it's not him." Afterward, he became disheartened for many months.

Nghĩa had been transferred to the South. His father lost his strength and grew weaker as a result. He had a small ulcer on his back that developed into something more serious. The hospital didn't have enough beds or medicine, so his mother took his father home to care for him instead. Due to his father's health condition, his parents didn't feel the need to evacuate to the countryside, so they remained in the city and took their chances with the American bombings instead. Aerial bombardments shook people's homes so violently that plaster flaked off walls. The city's electrical grid went down for many consecutive days, so it was pitch-black at night and stifling hot during the day. His mother would stay up to fan his father. His father's pain was so debilitating that he vomited all the medicine she gave him. In his last week, his father seemed to get better, and he forced himself to sit up and eat rice. However, he couldn't sleep for several days. He said he wanted to stay awake through the night until he died. Night eventually came, and his mother boiled him a pot of hot tea. She helped him relax at a table under a window. Under the cover of darkness, a city was at war, and here his father awaited death. He expelled his last breath early the next morning, gently holding his wife's hand. He slumped in his chair and whispered the name of his youngest son, Nghĩa.

Tân's mother never wrote about any of these things in her letters when he and his other siblings were abroad. She didn't mention it later in her life, either. Now, as Tân goes through the trunk, he realizes that their mother had written to her youngest son about the contents of those old letters. *You are unlucky to be born during a time of war,* she wrote in a letter dated December 31, 1972. The world was on fire then, the city a wasteland, yet Tân's mother steadfastly remained in Hà Nội. The bombardment threw up debris that shattered glass windows, but his mother sat in the exact spot where her husband used to sit. As though he were alive, she would boil a pot of tea and place it between two tiny cups on the tray. One letter went:

> Last night, the exploding bombs felt so close, but Linh, a girl living downstairs, ran up and sat with me by the window. She was your classmate—maybe you remember her, Nghĩa? Linh will be graduating from the Military University of Medical Studies and soon heading to the South, too.
>
> She said she wants to go there to be with you. I still remember the day you left for the South. Both you and Linh were just children then. But she's all grown up now, a beautiful and courageous soldier. When I look back at my life, I treasure giving birth to both sons and daughters. But now, seeing the destruction everywhere, it might have been better had you been born a daughter. In times of war, even daughters may not be spared, but at least a daughter wouldn't keep her parents in the dark. I know in my heart that you are still alive, but where are you now, my beloved son? How can you remain silent for so long? Not a word from you, not a single letter for me. Tell me, why is that, my dear son, Nghĩa?

My dear son, Nghĩa! Those are the last words Tân's mother wrote to her youngest son. No more letters appeared after that date, and none in 1973. Peace had been restored by then. Tân and his siblings took turns coming home after their successful education abroad.

Tân's mother, who gave birth to prosperous children, should have been the happiest of mothers. Yet in her entire life she rarely experienced happiness. Her face, until the day she died, was always one of longing, heartbreak, and inconsolable loss. Like those letters she had kept deep inside the trunk next to her bed, her sorrow was never voiced, a sorrow known deeply to her alone. At least the grief of the old professes the dignity of not calling attention to itself—to have been aware of such pain would tear your heart in two and make your life not worth living.

301

Had we gone all the way to Nha Trang instead of stopping to rest, no one would have been the wiser. But our vehicle pulled up in front of a coffee shop at the entrance to a small town. And if I hadn't heard that song playing, there would have been no reason for me to go inside. Someone turned the cassette player off just as I entered, but I knew I had heard a war anthem playing, not one of those melodramatic numbers that most places played nowadays.

The coffee shop was called Lucuma, its name written on a plank of wood, located on the first floor of a three-story house with a mossy-green roof. Though the coffee shop itself occupied the central room, patrons most likely sat out in the garden. I greeted the barista behind the counter and ordered a cup of black coffee, then made my way out the back door toward the garden area.

A wind gusted through the trees that afternoon. The spacious garden was full of green lucuma and star apple trees. A hodge-podge of rattan tables and chairs were arranged under the foliage along the pebble paths. I was the only customer there. Birds warbled overhead. I thought it would take some time for the driver to repair our vehicle. Exhausted, I sat down and closed my eyes.

"Sir, your coffee," a voice said softly.

I hadn't heard the woman's footsteps. She had approached me without making a sound and placed a tray on my table. On the wooden platter sat a gorgeous antique cup and saucer, a silver-plated spoon, and a coffee strainer. I could smell my coffee and the Buôn Mê Thuột tea nearby.

"Your garden is beautiful," I said.

"Thank you, sir," the woman said politely in her soft southern accent. "You're always welcome here. Please come back again and enjoy our coffee."

"Of course."

"Sir," she went on, "is this your first time in town?"

"I guess you could say that. I was last here a very, very long time ago. Twenty-five years to be exact. We didn't have a lot of time to stay and relax back then as we were just passing through."

The woman seemed genuinely surprised by my answer. I looked at her sunless, narrow face and assumed that she was around forty, although her large and haunting eyes made her appear much younger. She caught me looking at her and glanced away shyly. After our brief encounter, she quietly retreated into the building. My eyes followed her as she left. Then it dawned on me: I realized why seeing her had stirred such an uncanny feeling in me. Certainly, I had never met this woman before, in fact no one even closely resembling her, yet I sensed that we knew each other somehow—that eerie feeling you get when strangers suddenly become very familiar to you. I returned my attention to the lucuma garden, the sky, and listened to the sounds they evoked. Overhead, I saw feathery clouds gathering and gently floating by. They gradually dissolved into the sky and turned everything around me pink. The weather was remarkably pleasant even now, as the day was coming to an end.

The wind picked up and whipped through the garden, sometimes softly and barely noticeable, and at other times more dramatically, reminding me of an orchestral movement. A green-and-brown leaf fell off a star apple tree and landed near my coffee cup. I abandoned my unfinished coffee where it was, stood up, and left the table. I wanted to take another good look at the woman, the one who gave me such a strange, hard-to-place feeling.

Nobody was in the shop when I walked in. I approached the counter and observed an ice machine, some overripe mangoes, a blender, jars of sugar, jars of coffee, and a glass case containing cigarettes. Behind the counter, in a dark corner, a picture hung on the wall. It wasn't a painting at all, but a framed and enlarged photograph of a tank. I was sure it wasn't an M48 Patton. I couldn't see the photo clearly, but I knew right away that it was a T54 tank camouflaged with leaves.

I went behind the counter and turned on the light. I froze in my tracks when I saw Toàn, Trung, and Chí in the black-and-white photo. The lighting wasn't very good and the photo had faded over time, but without a doubt the men in the photo were them. That tank—301—was indeed ours. In the photo, Toàn wore a headband and had an AK-47 slung across his chest. He was carrying an NSV machine gun. Trung and Chí were leaning against the turret with their arms draped over each other's shoulders. Their backs must have covered the numbers, but the tank's star emblem was clear as day. All three looked incredibly young, and not one of them very photogenic. Their features were slightly blurry, but I couldn't mistake their smiles for anyone else's. Seeing the photo brought back such a wave of emotions that I found it hard to breathe. I trembled and felt my throat closing up.

I heard someone's wooden clogs coming down the staircase, but I kept my eyes on the photo. As the afternoon sun vanished and the room grew silent, a woman appeared behind the counter. Somewhere far off a train whistled and shortly after that it rumbled through town, shaking the ground a little. A wall clock announced the top of the hour. I recalled the war song I had overheard earlier when our vehicle stopped. All sorts of scenarios raced through my mind. I turned my body around slowly and faced the woman. She leaned her elbows on the counter and rested her face on her open palms. She had fine features and looked unassuming. Though her beauty had faded through time, her spell had not. She looked at me kindly.

"You know what?" I said hesitantly. "It's kind of strange. That tank in the photo used to be mine."

"Heavens, it's you," she answered, lowering her voice. "I almost didn't recognize you because it's been so long. But, you know, I always believed that you'd come back some day."

•

In 1975, on the last morning of March, a coastal town once crowded with people emptied out overnight. When I first heard about it, I still wasn't sure whether to believe that Buôn Mê Thuột had actually fallen. Artillery fire was coming from the direction of Khánh Dương. At first, only small clusters of people escaped down from the mountains, but then many others followed. There were rumors going around that parachuters had come to defend the Ma Đơ Rắc Pass, hoping to stop the Việt Cộng and recapture Đắk Lắk within a few days. But the evacuation, part of the overall exit strategy, ended up killing a lot more people instead. The coastal town, once peaceful, was now a dangerous and chaotic place. Buses, military trucks, civilians with their belongings, and defeated soldiers carrying weapons swarmed the roads, taking Highways 1 and 21. A huge stampede followed. Then looting, raping, fighting, people trampling each other. It was as though the world were ending. The defense line on the pass was overrun. Surviving ARVN soldiers in red berets held their bloody heads while retreating. Throngs of soldiers ran with their machine guns. Shoeless and shirtless, they looked like gorillas. Terrified, they smothered their fellow comrades in a mad scramble through town. The town itself was eventually razed to the ground by NVA artillery and tanks. NVA infantrymen would completely overrun the area and slaughter everyone. For a month the town descended into lawlessness, and by the end, it seemed as though the whole world were on fire.

Around noon, airplanes flew in from the sea and bombed Dục Mỹ to push back the enemy. Mortar and plaster shook from the walls; glass windows were broken and shattered. By early evening, gunfire filled the air along the neighborhoods and the beachfront, seemingly from every direction. The shooting stopped around midnight. Finally, on the following morning, the gunfire died down completely. A red sun crept on the horizon, revealing the vast sea beyond.

•

The owner of the Lucuma photography studio and his daughter sat patiently in their unlit house. They had locked themselves inside but couldn't take their eyes off the scene unfolding beyond the window. The sun crested the sea in all its brilliance. They heard the attack by the NVA's revolutionaries and the opposing ARVN soldiers retreating just outside. The father was anxious. He could have left two weeks earlier but decided to stay because he wasn't sure how things would turn out. He couldn't afford to lose his house, his garden, or his business. Now that he needed to make a decision, the evacuation, even though it was voluntary, sounded like a bad idea to him. The daughter requested her father's permission to remain at the house, saying that she would rather die than risk her life on such a dangerous escape. So they stayed hidden in their photography studio. Soldiers ransacked their neighborhood but by some stroke of luck didn't discover their studio. Their shop sign was riddled with bullets but the walls remained standing. Had the mayhem continued, looters wouldn't have left the studio intact, but only by the grace of God was their fate decided.

The bright sky that day stirred the whole region awake. Crashing waves, however, wasn't what roused people from sleep, but the reverberation of tanks rumbling along the ground like the foreshocks of an impending earthquake.

"Be careful!" the terrified father cried out. "They're here! Stay away from the door!"

A column of nearly a dozen T54 and K63 tanks roared down the road, heading south, pummeling everything in their path. Their treaded wheels rolled along the cracked surface of the road. The townsfolk were terrified of the howling turrets. Houses shook violently and the smell of diesel choked the air.

The town was liberated within less than five hours. As the tanks continued on past the town, the ones in front began to vanish into the southern horizon. The sky was blue again along the coast. A sense of normalcy returned.

"It sounds like they're right outside," the father said.

"Dear Lord, they are," the daughter said. "I can see one trying to turn its engine off."

They heard soldiers jumping off the tank. The men talked in a northern accent. They shouted, laughed, and teased each other. A loud sound followed. Curious about the scene unfolding outside, the girl approached the window and peered through the parted curtain. The tank abruptly sputtered to life, discharging a plume of black smoke, then fell quiet. The soldiers lifted up the hatch and slammed it closed again. A few minutes later, their tank restarted. The girl covered her ears as the floor trembled beneath her feet. Smoke discharged into the air. When she uncovered her ears, the deafening engine had stopped. She heard heavy footsteps approaching. Her father, frightened by what was happening, turned pale and fled upstairs to find a place to hide. A series of successive knocks on the door sounded like gunshots. She stood frozen in a corner.

"Nobody's here," came a voice. "The photographer must've run off."

"I'm sure I just saw somebody at the window," another voice said. "Could be a parachuter inside. I'll check it out."

The daughter was mortified, but there was little choice but to step forward and unlock the door. "Hello, sirs," she muttered.

The two men who stood outside the door returned her greeting. This was the first time she had seen Việt Cộng soldiers in the flesh. One was brawny, had short-cropped hair, and towered over the other. A rifle was slung over his shoulder, and he was carrying a plastic can in one hand. The other was diminutive and bamboo thin. He wore a headband and also carried a gun. When he saw that it was a girl who opened the door, he quickly lowered his weapon. The men's hands, faces, and military fatigues were black with soot and smoke.

The men told her they needed to stop to repair their tank, but that they wouldn't take long. However, they had run out of potable water. They politely asked her if they could have some water before they returned to the road. The soldiers were extremely affable and considerate, which gave the girl conflicting feelings, making her feel both confused by them and somehow strangely comforted at the same time. She invited them inside and said that they could get as much water as they needed from the water tank at the back of the photography studio, and if they wished to get cleaned up, they could do that, too. But the men said they didn't have time to wash up and only needed to fill up their plastic can. They carried weapons and were covered from head to toe in filth, but they didn't come across to her as being typical soldiers. They were in fact nice, decent men. At the very least, they didn't rummage through her house or pry into her life. Although they were in a hurry, they loitered for a little while after filling up their water can, so she offered them tea. The soldiers sat down to drink it.

Maintaining friendly appearances, they struck up a conversation, complimenting her garden out back, her elegant photography studio, the excellent tea, and the photos she had displayed in the glass cabinet. They also told her a massive army was coming to the area soon, complete with infantrymen, combat trucks, and tanks.

"Don't be frightened by the sight," one man said. "Just live your life as normal as possible and keep your studio open. The NVA will run the enemy out of town quickly, and the war will very likely be over soon. Probably within this year, or maybe even before that, during this dry season we can reach Cà Mau."

"I can't wait until we're done with this," the small-framed soldier wearing the headband said, slumping back in his chair. "When there are no more Americans, no more ARVN, and no more bombing and gunfire, our country will be reunified. I would regret nothing if I had only one day to live to witness just that."

"What are you talking about?" the other soldier frowned. "Be careful what you say."

"Don't take it the wrong way," the first one said. "I've seen a lot so far in this war, so it'd be a waste if I died before reunification. I have to live long enough at least to enjoy a moment of peace. And do you know what else? When this war is over, I'm thinking about becoming a bus driver. Wouldn't it be great to drive around the country? I'll get to see all the mountains, rivers, and rice fields after years of living and fighting in the deep jungle. I'll get to see our new socialist country. And of course, I'll come back here every year to visit this place, this house, and our new friend sitting right here."

Because of their northern accents, the girl didn't quite understand what they were saying. She remained quiet. Every now and then, she meekly nodded, said yes, and glanced at the ground. The way the soldiers were acting made her feel less nervous and less scared. Her apprehension soon vanished altogether, and there was no need to stay vigilant. All her prejudices about the soldiers were gone, and she felt surprised at her own gullibility. Nobody brainwashed her. It dawned on her that they were by no means the bloodthirsty killers or arsonists she'd imagined. The newspapers and the radio often portrayed the Việt Cộng as stoic and emotionless figures, men who were uncompromising and cruel, indecent men full of themselves. But these men were courteous and behaved sincerely.

The soldiers looked around and noticed a pack of cigarettes and a lighter her father had left behind on the table. The ashtray was overflowing with cigarette butts. They saw a man's coat hanging on a hook. The two Việt Cộng soldiers, of course, knew that she wasn't alone and that there was someone else living in the house, but they didn't interrogate her. Instead, they asked about her parents, but when she hesitated to give them an answer, they didn't press further. Honestly, now that they were here, she didn't understand the fear she had felt toward the communists, a fear that overshadowed not only her life and her father's, but also the lives of the other people in her town. It was ridiculous that her father was so terrified by the communists' arrival that he ran upstairs and hid, leaving her behind to deal with them herself. She imagined his face turning pale, his body trembling in some dark, hidden alcove upstairs, worrying that the communists would go looking for him.

But the communist soldiers had more important business to attend to. They glanced at their watches, quickly stood up, and slung their guns over their shoulders. They said goodbye, thanked her again, and shook her hand. One soldier barely touched her hand before letting go of it; the other took his time and held her soft hand in his rough one for longer.

"We are just soldiers," the latter man said, "so next time don't call us *sirs*, please. We'll be back. I'll never forget this place and this morning. Your hometown now has been liberated. Look how calm and beautiful it is outside. After today, I get to go back to my coastal hometown, Quảng Ninh, but I consider all coastal towns my hometown, so, in a way, we aren't strangers because of our kinship—we are both coastal people." Finally, he let go of her hand.

The two soldiers returned to their tank. The girl then hurried outside with a camera in her hands. She ran to the front of the tank. They had already started the engine, and the tank sputtered to life but didn't move yet. Its various hatches opened and three men emerged from the idling tank. The girl's tiny, fragile body shuddered next to the enormous piece of machinery, which was shaking violently and heating up. The driver let the engine run, causing the tank to thunderously roar to life. The girl wasn't a photographer—her father was—so she rarely had a chance to use the camera. She bit her lip and mustered enough courage to ask the men to pose for a picture. After the camera clicked, she realized that she had used up the last picture of the roll. She told the men to wait while she went back inside to find another camera, but when she came back out, the tank was already rumbling away in a cloud of dust. Standing in the middle of the road with her Kodak in hand, she looked on as the T54 tank sped away from her. The tank appeared smaller and far less intimidating at this distance, its top shaking in the wind as it glistened under the sun.

•

The days of upheaval eventually passed and a new chapter in our lives began. But those who felt nostalgic for life before 1975 fled the country on fishing boats—one of whom was the proprietor of the photography studio. His daughter stayed behind. She settled in the house surrounded by her lucuma garden. The studio closed down, but she opened a coffee shop in its place. Occasionally, old clients stopped by to claim their photos. Although groups of soldiers also passed through, none were the men in the photo. Over the years, more and more soldiers were discharged, but the photo of the tank remained unclaimed.

Time marched on. The girl got married and had children. In the postwar years, her life became more difficult and she aged more quickly. Her husband, having left their poor town, found work in Nha Trang. Her children, now grown up, also left. She wanted to follow them but couldn't bear to leave her hometown. Instead, she lived alone in the house cocooned in her lucuma garden and struggled to make ends meet. The only remnant of her former photography studio was the faded photo of the tank.

•

Day after day and year after year, the house stood along the main street. It was as though the house was yearning for another future, an ache that was finally abated when I, one of the former crew members, recognized the tank.

I wasn't one of the three men in the photo but an NSV machine gunner on the same tank. The woman had mistaken me for one of those soldiers she had met. After surviving the battle on Ma Đơ Rắc Pass, I crossed Dục Mỹ safely, but one night I was injured by gunfire on Road 21. My injury wasn't debilitating, but I couldn't fight for over ten days. After I left the hospital, not yet fully recovered, I commandeered a Jeep abandoned on the roadside and caught up to Tank 301.

I drove through several cities and towns: Ninh Hòa, Nha Trang, and Cam Ranh. I drove up the Ngoạn Mục Pass, pushed through Di Linh and Đức Trọng, and then headed south to Bảo Lộc and Lộc Ninh, finally reaching Sài Gòn. On April 30, 1975, I was still following the tread marks that Tank 301 left behind on its route. After passing Lăng Cha Cả, I drove to the Tân Sơn Nhất Airport but didn't see my tank anywhere. We declared victory that same rainy afternoon.

Without giving up hope, I returned to Lăng Cha Cả and Cầu Bông. I even made it to Phan Rang—the well-known battlefield on our way to attack and seize Sài Gòn—but Tank 301 never appeared. What had happened to me wasn't a fluke but the work of some higher power. For twenty years I had looked for my tank, and not until now, no longer the young man I was, did I finally get to see the photo of my fellow comrades. That afternoon, standing in front of the photo of our tank, both the woman and I couldn't hold in our emotions any longer. We wept as we revisited our experiences from twenty years ago, shedding our tears in memory of that war.

Letters from the Year of the Water Buffalo

Nights were short in the dry seasons back in those days, seasons unlike any I've lived through since. I remember how agreeable the weather was, how nature seemed to lie deep in her slumber. The December sky was clear, and when January came, eggplant flowers blossomed in the cool, crisp air, announcing the onset of a new year. At night, schools of buffalo fish, splashing about, swam upstream to lay eggs in the Đắc Bờ Là River, leaving in their wake waves that rippled outward in perfect circles. The water, gently lapping against the shore, remained calm. At night, as it was the dry season, the cool southeasterly winds carried in from far away the hope of joy and reconciliation, rustling the leaves in the woods and uplifting the hearts of men.

The sky brightened as the sun rose over the eastern shore of the Đắc Bờ Là River. The mist rolling off the water softly dissipated beneath the cobalt sky, and darkness gradually faded away to reveal patches of rosy clouds above. The morning wind exhaled deeply while a scarlet sun, burning glorious and bright, seemed to levitate in the air. The land around the river, its mountains and hills, stirred from sleep. Life, engulfed by fire—and full of suffering, sorrow, and despair—nevertheless had the resolve to carry on.

That day, I looked up and saw a white-naped yuhina darting in the sky. Dawn comes earlier than usual in the dry season, the sky peaceful and bright, and without the sound of artillery. On that morning, however, I felt a pang in my heart, an inexplicable ache whose source I couldn't locate. At first, I thought the pain arose from a dream, from something more imagined and fantastical. But according to the schedule, at this very moment, the artillery battery at the special quarter 24 and Bãi Ủy military base was supposed to fire. Subsequently, more M101 howitzers, one after another, unleashed their terrifying, thunderous payloads into the air. The clear dawn was immediately drowned in thick, dark smoke.

This was how a typical day on Hill 400 started. But this was only the beginning. American bombs would rain down endlessly before the day was over. Sometimes the sky filled with bombers, flying either in pairs or alone. They would hover for a long time above us like a Ferris wheel. Then suddenly, tilting and banking down, they screamed through the sky. Their bombs glistened under the sun and grew larger before the inevitable impact. You could count to five before the bombs struck the hill. Rocks and earth were blasted from hillsides, leaving scars across the land. Air raid trenches and defensive forts shook violently. Each of the Douglas AD-6 Skyraiders carried anywhere from ten to twenty bombs, but during each run, each plane dropped only one or two. Sometimes four napalm bombs fell on the A side of Hill 400, drowning the whole land in a sea of fire. After the bomber pilots flew away, the gunners came in, then the artillery, tanks, and infantrymen finally entered. For over a month this series of events happened without interruption. The enemy either bombed the hill or fired on it with their artillery and followed with a ground attack from the B side of the hill.

Our defense post on the A side of the hill was almost taken over by the enemy more than once. Their strike force, looking disheveled in their open shirts, carried bayoneted rifles and bravely risked their lives. They would rush our trenches and toss their M26 grenades in. We used every ounce of energy we had to push back the enemy. Nearly every day, the hillsides were covered with corpses. At night, we cleared out the battlefield for the most part, but by the following morning, the stench of corpses stacked atop one another was inescapable. All kinds of ARVN soldiers, including parachuters and special task force troops, took turns attacking our platoon, and many men died right there along the hill's slope. Around the time of the Tết holiday, several enormous men of Regiment 52 in skull insignia decisively attacked our platoon.

By nighttime, as though a truce were agreed upon, neither we nor the enemy fired on Hill 400. This gave us time to restock our military supplies, eat dinner, welcome reinforcements, and take the wounded and the dead down from the hill. We also used the time to dig combat trenches and build air raid shelters to replace the ones that had been destroyed earlier by bombing. On the other side of the hill, the enemy was also digging trenches, repairing their damaged infrastructure, tending to the wounded, and collecting corpses. In the darkness, we heard people crying out in pain like ghosts as they struggled miserably to live. The land looked hellish and apocalyptic, the hillsides spotted with corpses and the accompanying shadows of laborers digging holes. We clung to our guns but didn't shoot the pitiful gravediggers, although they often came close enough for us to shoot. For anyone to witness such suffering without end was heartbreaking. The injuries and deaths inflicted upon our enemy neither comforted nor titillated us.

During long nights of fighting along the banks of the Đắc Bờ Là River, Boeing B-52 Stratofortresses flashed their lights overhead and emitted terrifying, explosive sounds. By morning, the ghosts of war roused from their beds. Shelling, bombing, and waves of attacks had killed several people. The combatants of Regiment 53 were demoralized and exhausted, but they followed their commander's orders. Clenching their jaws, the soldiers showed determination and charged ahead, sacrificing themselves in the process. This didn't seem like war, but more like a mass suicide. It was an extraordinary scene.

Then, unexpectedly, on the 23rd of December of the lunar calendar, a week prior to the Tết holiday, silence fell over the land. No artillery, no bombs. Maybe the war had ended, or it had been plunged into an abyss, although the front lines remained exactly where they were before. We still occupied the A side of the hill, the enemy the B side. It seemed we had reached a stalemate, without a victor for either side. No planes flew overhead, no cannons fired. All the fires were extinguished, causing the ground to cool quickly. The battlefield, now empty of sound, looked as tranquil as a pastoral painting.

The sky remained blue and cloudless during the three days of Tết; the weather turned in spectacular fashion. Hope for peace resonated through the air, appeared luminous under the sun, and was amplified by the winds. Though peace was elusive, all of us felt its presence as though we could touch it with our hands. At the bottom of the hill, the Đắc Bờ Là River's blue waters bubbled calmly, winding through the river's many twists and turns.

The flag of the National Liberation Front of South Việt Nam on the A side of the hill, planted atop one of the combat trenches, flapped in the wind. The ARVN flag fluttered and could be heard rustling all the way on our side. We saluted our flag when the sun rose in the morning, when fog still lingered in the air. The enemy saluted their flag later in the day, after the sun had reached its zenith in the sky. Slowly, they pulled their flag to the top of a tall and shiny aluminum pole while singing:

> Oh citizens! At our fatherland's call,
> With one heart we go forth,
> And give our lives gladly . . .

On this idyllic morning, the world seemed to dissolve into thin air, and even the anthem that the South Vietnamese soldiers were singing didn't sound awful to us. The way they stood at attention and sang the anthem gallantly didn't bother me at all. In my eyes, the young comrades whose voices rose in unison were not the abhorrent enemy; rather, they were "the other side."

"We're all Vietnamese, descendants of the legendary Lạc Hồng. We have been fighting and killing each other, but from now on let's swear that we'll never shoot each other senselessly again." The commander of the ARVN soldiers on the B side of the hill, Second Lieutenant Duy, had said those kind words while he was intoxicated on the morning of the first day of Tết.

The ARVN soldiers' goodwill started three days ago. The number of soldiers in each platoon remained the same at fifteen. All the combatants who occupied the hill had withdrawn. The tanks were gone, too. The hillsides no longer had the stench of corpses, and grass even grew in a few places. The gully between the hills used to be flooded with human blood up to one's calves, but now soldiers from both sides built a simple thatched-roof bamboo house and called it the House of Harmony. The house represented the ceasefire agreement. Opposing battalion commanders came to celebrate its grand opening.

Since the evening before Tết, the house had become a meeting place. Each side assigned four people to defend their position, and the rest went into the gully to celebrate Tết. It was like two teams of a soccer game. No one came armed. At first, the soldiers were cautious, so they sat with their own comrades, but later, without anyone's order, everybody commingled and had a great time. Both sides prepared delicious food—traditional food for Tết such as *bánh chưng*, *bánh tét*, and wild vegetables, and fish caught in the Đắc Bờ Là River. Our side contributed Chinese, Thai, and Russian food, alcohol, and cigarettes; the other side provided American canned food, alcohol, and more cigarettes. We offered them Điện Biên cigarettes, and they offered us Ruby Queen cigarettes in return.

Soldiers at the party were young and handsome, sunburnt but in high spirits, though they also appeared emaciated from the constant fighting. At the party, everybody loosened up and enjoyed celebrating the peaceful New Year, interacting cheerfully without mentioning the war. We talked about our hometowns and how we were all soldiers who had to be away from home during Tết. No arguments, no arrogance, no unpleasant behavior. Our hearts softened. There was only goodwill, sincerity, and a sense of fellowship. We showed an indescribable empathy and understanding for each other. Before we said our goodbyes, Thanh, the designated singer of my platoon, sang "Việt Nam: Our Beautiful Country." A designated singer from the other side sang "A Flock of Vietnamese Birds" and "Our Hands Make a Big Circle." We sang some songs together, and some of the men even cried. Hatred should be abolished, not heightened, I thought.

I will never forget the "peace of 1973" and the unfathomable, tragic days that followed Tết that year.

After the night of New Year's Eve, we had a few more gatherings in the House of Harmony. I can still remember the faces, names, and personalities of all the soldiers on the other side. Among them was Second Lieutenant Duy, someone whose features, stature, and voice I can describe clearly even many years later. Duy was three years older than me and had been fighting the war for longer, but he hadn't aged as quickly as I had. He was tall with a fair complexion. His voice was deep, but he didn't talk much. Although he kept mostly to himself, he was a good-natured and thoughtful person. His subordinates respected him. Duy said he was Catholic and had moved to the South from Hà Nội. I wasn't afraid of him. Had we met under more reasonable conditions, Duy was the kind of person I easily would have befriended. He seemed to like me as well. We didn't say much, but deep down inside I think we trusted each other. We talked about ourselves and asked questions to get to know the other better.

"Are you familiar with Hà Nội?" he asked.

"No, but my village isn't far from there," I said. "There's a river that separates my village from Hà Nội. I enlisted to fight at eighteen, so I haven't had the chance to go visit the city yet."

"My father left Hà Nội to relocate our family to the South in 1954." Duy sighed. "I was just a kid back then, but I still have vague memories of my cousins. The house that we used to live in together was very beautiful, located in Khuông Việt District. It now belongs to my uncle. In 1954, my uncle would rather live far away from God and relatives than leave Hà Nội."

"That doesn't sound that bad. Once this war is all over, you can visit your relatives up North."

"It'll be difficult, even if our country restores peace." Duy smiled and shook his head. "It's hard to tell if the North and South will ever have normalized relations again."

Duy grew up in Hố Nai, near Sài Gòn. After high school, he studied at the Thủ Đức Military Academy and became an officer. He was away from his family every year during Tết. He drunkenly showed me a picture of his girlfriend. "I wish I could send you and your comrades a wedding invitation when we get married, so you guys can come visit us in the South," he added.

Although we tried to avoid talking about the ongoing war, sometimes it slipped from our tongues. My E24 and his E53 infantry regiments had encountered each other on several occasions. It was a bloody fight every time. On Hill 400, prior to our ceasefire, Duy's company had to refill his ranks three times.

"My best friend, Lieutenant Sáng, was killed right here, just before the ceasefire," Duy said, glancing down at the dirt floor.

Once, Duy himself didn't have time to withdraw with his men after their attack was repelled by our heavy machine guns. He had hidden in a bomb crater from morning until night. The crater was very close to our combat trench.

"If I had a grenade," Duy said and made a fist, "your heavy machine guns would have been destroyed completely."

While he was drunk, Duy even threatened us. "The hill your men are occupying insults us, so be ready when we strike back."

Despite what he said, I didn't feel nervous. Duy was the commander of the opposing army, but he was a noble and gentle man. In fact, although we knew each other for less than a week, I felt a tinge of sadness when we said goodbye. I would be transferred to a scout battalion and Duy would be put on leave. In the House of Harmony, Duy showed me the official papers for his departure.

"I'm very lucky. I can breathe a sigh of relief now. I've been feeling so nervous for the past few days. I was born in the Year of the Water Buffalo, and next month is supposed to be my unlucky month. But here I am, getting shot at every day," he said.

"But we've reached a truce, haven't we?" I asked.

"Yes, you're right," Duy sighed, closing his eyes. "But a soldier like me, who doesn't get to choose when he lives or dies, can't predict anything. Honestly, it's pretty extraordinary that they're putting me on leave. I can't believe it myself."

Duy invited us to stay for a going-away party that his platoon would throw for him. We politely declined the invitation, but each took a shot of alcohol to congratulate him on his leave.

"What about your side?" Duy asked. "When can you get out of here based on the condition 'one in, one out'?"

"No idea," I answered. "One of these days, I guess. Hopefully soon."

"I'm asking because I want a favor from you. It's about my family, you see . . . "

"Tell me what you have in mind." I was surprised. "If I can do it, I'll help."

"Like I said the other day, my uncle lives in Hà Nội. For the last twenty years, we haven't heard anything from him, but my father always thinks about him, especially during Christmas or Tết. A few days ago, there was some news about the signing of the Paris Peace Accords, so my father wrote me a long letter where he talked about his hope for peaceful reunification, but he sounded very sad. He talked about his brother and memories of the North. He wrote that he wished there was a way for him to exchange correspondence with my uncle. Well, now you probably understand why I need your help. I've written my uncle a letter. It's short, and I told him briefly how my family is doing in the South. That's it. Please read it. If you're kind enough to help me, my father would be delighted."

I mulled over his offer in my head. I was torn by his request and thought it strange that he wanted help with delivering the letter, but it was hard for me to say no. What would Duy and other ARVN soldiers think about the communists' kindness or lack thereof?

Duy became very emotional, his hands trembling as he handed me the letter and, with his voice verging on becoming tearful, he thanked me. He even gave me a half-hearted hug.

But I still felt anxious. Earlier in the day, I saw soldiers on the B side of the hill stand in formation and salute the flag. I counted fifteen men total. I wondered if another officer had been sent to replace Duy, or if they had decided to keep him after all, though it shouldn't have bothered me either way.

I left Hill 400 and followed a worn path along the riverbanks on my way to the battalion headquarters. I took my time, walking leisurely, and removed the letter from my pocket. Duy's uncle's name and address were written on the slender, handmade envelope: *13 Khuông Việt District, Hà Nội.* The white envelope had a letter inside written on brittle pelure paper. He had forgotten to seal the envelope all the way. I thought about reading the letter, but then decided not to and put it back in my pocket. I would enclose Duy's letter with my own correspondence to my family before mailing it; I would ask my younger brother to hand the letter to Duy's uncle in person. But then I thought, what if the policy of "one in, one out" becomes a reality? The battalion will be transferred to the North and I'll be allowed to take my leave. Then I can deliver the letter myself. Duy's uncle will be thrilled. But why does Khuông Việt District sound so unfamiliar? Where's it located?

I soaked in the natural beauty around me and began to daydream. The surrounding land murmured under the vast indigo sky. I left my platoon in the morning. By three o'clock in the afternoon, the enemy had launched an unexpected offensive. The sun was high in the sky and luminous, but not one of my soldiers saw the attack coming. My platoon's combat trenches were wiped out, which gave us little chance of countering the offensive. What was happening? Had our sentries fallen asleep? I never found out. Even Thanh, the only survivor of the attack, knew nothing. He had come down with a fever and was resting in a trench when he heard the patter of feet. He looked out and saw that the ARVN soldiers had already swarmed the battlefield. Thanh, staggering toward me at the back side of the hill, leaned his bloody and beaten face against my chest, and cried.

Our battalion commander ordered us to launch a counterattack to regain control of Hill 400. It was our fault that this was happening. As a result, I was dismissed as commander of my platoon and demoted from sergeant major to private. I accepted the disciplinary action, but this didn't exclude me from participating in the counteroffensive.

"We'll retaliate and get our revenge . . ." I blurted, but the words got caught in my throat.

If we wanted to recapture our position while a large number of the enemy troops were occupying the hill, we would have to launch a similar surprise offensive. However, this wasn't possible during the day. Our battalion commander came up with a plan for attack: we would secretly move on the enemy at dawn. The plan would not involve a lot of men, maybe only a small group armed with submachine guns and hand grenades. They would advance up the hill from the gully at midnight. After launching the attack, they would recapture both the A and B positions on the hill.

At first light, we were waiting in the gully between the hills. The House of Harmony was still there, its thatched roof still visible even after all the explosive projectiles we used on it. The ARVN soldiers had expected our counterattack at night, but nothing happened so they became less vigilant. We waited until the sun was high in the sky and the fog had lifted, around the time when Duy's men normally saluted their flag, to launch an attack.

From the central location of the House of Harmony, we advanced on the enemy. Our battalion commander was in charge of securing the B side of the hill, and I was in charge of the A side. We inched forward without making noise. My heart was thumping so loudly that I couldn't hear the sound of my own footsteps or the footsteps of my comrades behind me. The prelude to the counterattack was like the calm before a storm. We said nothing to each other until we reached the enemy's combat trench.

"Now . . . !" came a voice.

Grenades exploded.

The enemy soldiers were eating and they, along with their food, were blasted through the air. They would now have to fight us hand to hand. Sounds of howling, grunts, punches, and people getting gored filled the air. We cut down the enemy with our AK-47s. Grenades detonated throughout their trench. We recaptured the B side of the hill within ten minutes; the A side took even less time.

Afterward, I walked to the opposing commander's bunker and took down their flag. Their bunker had been obliterated by grenades, like a casket with its lid blown off. Trays of food, alcohol, and canned rations were strewn everywhere. Three people who were in the trench, their bodies entangled, had died together. One of them was slumped against the dirt wall. I threw aside the metal helmet covering the corpse's face. I took a step back, shocked by what I saw. It was Second Lieutenant Duy! His lopsided head revealed a pair of wide, open eyes; blood was pouring out of his mouth. I didn't know what to say. What's going on here? Did this mean his leave was revoked? Or was there even a leave at all?

Somehow among the smoke-filled, bloody bunker of corpses a PRC-25 radio survived. The radio emitted a blue light, and I could hear orders from their high command coming through the head-phones still looped around one of the soldier's necks. He lay dead next to Duy. The urgent orders were angry and threatening, full of curses. Whoever was on the other end must have forgotten all the secret codes.

I plucked the PRC-25 from the gnarled fingers of the corpse. I was surprised at myself when I blurted loudly into the headset, "Fuck you, Americans."

•

Many years have passed since that time, but the sorrows stemming from the events of 1973 still haunt my memories. Sometimes, during Tết, I revisit the memory of Hill 400. I remember how the waters of the Đắc Bờ Là River glistened and refracted in the early morning light. Although I know it's only a dream, my heart is torn when I confront my fellow comrades who are already dead. Sometimes, in my dreams, I see Duy and remember him. But as time marches on, the way I remember him has changed. I feel no animosity or disgust toward him. In fact, what I feel is sympathy.

I never mailed Duy's letter to the North, as I had told him I would. I kept his letter at the bottom of my rucksack until the end of the war. After being discharged, I returned home. The letter stayed there among my many other things. Since there was no need for me to hang on to it anymore, I finally opened it. The envelope contained two letters, one to his uncle, dated 3rd day of Tết, 1973, in which he gave a greeting followed by a summary of his relatives' lives in the South. Duy had signed the let-ter with the postal code KBC. The other was much briefer, addressed to "Soldiers of the communist cause," and left unsigned. It read:

Dear NVA Soldiers,
Although I feel fortunate to take my leave, I'm worried about the rest of you. My commander has ordered us to seize the entire hill, which

will cause many of your people to die. The attack, one we have been urgently and gravely preparing for, will happen soon, if not this week then next. We plan to amass our troops. I don't want this to happen, but I have no other choice. Take care of yourselves, and please understand my brotherly concerns.

Later, I went to Hà Nội a few times and looked for Khuông Việt District but couldn't find it. I asked around but nobody knew. Some people guessed that it might have been the name of a small quarter under the French occupation. So I have kept Duy's letter to his uncle ever since. A letter from the Year of the Water Buffalo, 1973.

The Camp of the Seven Dwarfs

One afternoon, as darkness fell through the bamboo forest, I made my way along the Sa Thầy River from the February 3 logging camp[8] to the border defending post at A10. Markings in the grass became harder to see and the trees along the road's shoulder rustled in hushed, uneasy tones. I still had two hours left to go when, all at once, thunder clapped overhead—a tempest brewing—and I saw an ominous cloud rising over the barren hills east of the river. Before long, ribbons of clouds thickened above the river, turning the sky an inky purple. A strong wind whooshed through the humid air, bent trees, and flattened the reed beds along the riverbanks. The wind was so overpowering that the grasses seemed to flip straight toward the water. The crumbling rain lashed its swollen waves against the steep embankment. I lowered my head and ran, seeking shelter under a giant tree.

"Who's there?" a voice called out.

---

8   The camp is named for the date the Vietnamese Communist Party was founded, February 3, 1930.

I turned around. It was hard to make out who was in the storm, but I saw a figure nearby on the beaten path.

"Who's that?" he asked again, loudly.

"I'm a postal worker," I replied. "And you?"

A flash of lightning revealed a shadow emerging from the landscape. An immense, towering figure, shirtless, with a basket strapped to his back.

"Are you going to A10?" the stranger asked, advancing toward me.

"Yes," I answered, "but I got caught in this storm."

"We usually don't get these storms this time of year," he said. Then, he continued, "I'm a security guard at the logging camp." The wind and rain let up a little. "This will last for a while. You should come to my house and wait out the storm if you want. Follow me."

"Thank you," I said.

We slogged through the mud and entered a forested area. Thunder rumbled above the trees and, with the wind now to our backs, the storm finally subsided. I ducked under the branches and helped him brace his oversized back-basket. The forest thinned out and we reached a creek; we crossed a rickety bamboo bridge with handrails.

The stranger walked ahead and stopped to unlatch a gate. A pebbled path led us through a yard revealing an enormous bamboo-roofed house. Setting down his basket, he pushed the door open. We went inside the unlit house and I noticed the smell of incense used to keep mosquitos away.

"You can get undressed," he said, "since there's nobody here."

I put down my bag and began taking off my wet clothes.

"Hand them to me and I'll dry them," he said, adding, "Here's a towel."

He took my wet clothes and disappeared through the back door. As I was drying myself with the towel, he returned with a lighter. He approached the table and lit an American oil lamp, then set it down by the entryway.

"Put this on," he insisted, handing me a neatly folded soldier's uniform. "Will it fit?"

He was not the giant I had first imagined; in fact, he wasn't tall at all. He only came up to my shoulders. He was barrel-chested, with broad shoulders, which gave him a slightly stooped posture, reminding me of a bear cub. His arms and legs were stubby, too, though they looked strong. He was ugly, and his skin was dark and calloused. He frowned when I thanked him and said nothing. Afterward, he shut the door on his way out.

There was little to do that night since I was in the middle of a forest and it was raining outside, so I sat down on a bench near the table. Feeling bored, I looked around. The bamboo-roofed house had three rooms and an open ceiling, with no partition between the rooms. The place was well-kept and had few mosquitos, but the furniture was sparse, with only a table and bench arranged in the central room. On the wall hung a portrait of Hồ Chí Minh, a faded flag, and a banner with the slogan: *Everything is for the final victory*. The room to my right was mostly empty, with several machetes hanging on the wall and a spear leaning against one corner. On my left was a smaller room; it had a strange-looking bed with a plastic floral mat on it. There was no pillow. At the foot of the bed, above the window, was a shelf where a deflated, empty rucksack rested.

Feeling restless, I let out a deep breath and, not knowing what else to do, took out all the letters, newspapers, and magazines from the bag I had brought with me, laying them out on the table. I rearranged them and put them in order. The host returned and placed a plate of boiled manioc on the table.

"You must be sick of this food," he announced emphatically, "but it's all I have . . ."

"I'm not hungry."

We remained silent. Then he sat on the edge of the bench and turned slightly toward me.

"You have lots of letters," he remarked. "Are they all dry?"

"Yeah," I answered, looking at him suspiciously. "What's your name?"

"Mộc."

"Mộc . . . Mộc . . . " I said, tapping my temple. "Well, let me see. I left all the letters belonging to the February 3 logging camp at the headquarters. Maybe . . ."

"I don't get letters," he interrupted, "unless Heaven decides to write to me."

"Why don't you?" I asked, feeling surprised.

Mộc frowned and said nothing. The bad weather continued outside. I had wrapped everything in plastic bags, except for a *Military Arts and Literature* magazine, which I pushed toward him.

"I don't want it," he said in a mocking tone. "You can take it to the defending post for others to read. They need it more, and I can always borrow it from them later. Don't worry so much. The rain will stop by the time your clothes are dry. It won't be much longer. Storms don't last long this time of year."

"You must be very familiar with the weather here," I said.

"Of course. I've been living here for twenty years."

"Twenty years?" I was surprised to hear that.

"Every year for twenty years we've had a crop," Mộc went on. "In 1962, when I was in Pi Hà during Tết, I got a letter that my family had mailed out in early 1960. I know this because the postmark showed the location and date clearly, even though the letter itself was damaged because of the weather. I didn't hear any other news from my family until the end of 1966, when a guy from my village informed me of my mother's death in 1961. I also learned from him that my sister got married and moved to a coal mining town, and that my only brother joined the military and died somewhere in Laos in 1965."

"Where are you from?" I asked.

"Sơn Tây, Hòa Lạc, Thạch Thất District. I enlisted in 1959, at eighteen. I didn't return to my hometown again until 1977, eighteen years later. My village changed while I was gone, becoming a military airport." Mộc grew quiet. The rain lashed against the bamboo roof, cascading down the gutters. Cool air floated through the windows. A cricket chirped from some corner of the house. "Back then," he continued in his deep voice, "I wanted to go find my sister in Quảng Ninh. But it was during winter and my young daughter couldn't stand the cold in the North. We had no money, so it was impossible to stay. We returned here to the forest instead. I haven't gone back to the North since."

"Where's your daughter now?"

"I sent her to school in Đắc Tô not too long ago. She's boarding there. This is the first time we've been separated, but I don't have a choice. There's no school here and she's still illiterate at thirteen. I'm too busy to teach her, and it breaks my heart to have her living so far away. I look forward to hearing from her now and then. Maybe you can help me, because I don't want her letter to get lost."

"Where's your wife?" I asked.

"What?" he glowered. "Who?"

Surprised by his reaction, I apologized for my inappropriate question.

"Never mind," Mộc mumbled. "You don't have to apologize. It's all my fault. It has nothing to do with my wife and daughter." He went on, "I was a soldier when I first moved here. I had changed careers, but still lived here in this forest. How did I expect to find a wife for myself? I'm an old man, you know, and have no libido . . . " After some time deep in thought, he continued, "I joined the war in 1962, but for the past thirteen years I haven't left Sa Thầy. I've never actually fought on the battlefield. I'm a B3 pioneer soldier, but I've never seen an American. I'm over forty now and not as young as I used to be." Mộc tapped his fingers on the table and remained quiet for a moment. He said, "I got sick after I crossed the border. The fever almost killed me. My whole body was swollen; I thought I had leprosy and couldn't fight. If this had happened during the dry season, I would've been transferred to the North. But it was July, the rainy season, so my unit transferred me to Nua's defending post for treatment. That defending post is the house you're in now."

"Why is it called Nua's post?"

"Because he once lived here. His name was Y Nua, a member of the Êđê ethnic group." Mộc continued, "Y Nua was a jungle man. He built a cottage here after the Geneva Accords, living like a recluse, working the fields himself, and he offered a place for officials of the Kon Tum province to stay when they visited. There was never enough food to eat, though. He wore clothes made from bark and slept on a makeshift bed. My battalion came to the Central Highlands from Xê Nội, so his cottage became our first choice to set up a base camp. In 1962, during the wet season, there were five other sick soldiers besides me. Nua himself took care of us. By the next dry season, we had recovered and gone north. But on the afternoon before we left, Y Nua died in the field. A huge tree fell on him. After his burial, we decided to stay in the forest and continue his unfinished work. Working the fields is hard but not impossible, and it didn't take us long to get used to our job. When our regiment launched the first attack—the offensive in Plây-mơ-rông—in the dry season of 1963, there were six of us producing food for the soldiers. We've been farming since then."

Mộc bowed his head and breathed deeply. Outside, the storm quieted. Raindrops fell on the veranda and, in the stillness, shadows of drenched trees could be seen reflected off the window.

"The more Y Nua's place grows, the more difficulties we have to overcome. Living in isolation in the woods is the worst, but we got accustomed to it after several years. Not that it mattered, but there were times when nobody came here. We're B3 soldiers and we have to work hard to produce enough food for soldiers fighting out there beyond the forest. We haven't experienced much of the war. This place has never been bombed, so we've never seen B-52s or B-57s. Sometimes, a C-123 plane would spray chemicals on the forest. Although the foliage withered away, our farm was never affected.

Even when the American Division 4 launched a raid at the eastern side of Sa Thầy, we could only hear gunfire from here. We lived mostly unremarkable lives, but it's as though we've been forgotten, and we grow tired because of it. Farming is onerous, ravaging our bodies, and it has made us look old beyond our years. So the soldiers on the north side of B3, also known as Cánh Bắc, call this place the Camp of the Seven Dwarfs."

"The seven dwarfs?" I asked.

"Yeah. Seven—including Y Nua. I don't know why they call us dwarfs. But that's what this place is called now: the Camp of the Seven Dwarfs."

"Is there a Snow White?" I asked in all sincerity.

Mộc said nothing.

•

After a few minutes of silence, Mộc continued with his story:

We call it the Camp of the Seven Dwarfs, but we've lost nearly everyone. After Y Nua died, Tý followed him to the grave in 1964. The same kind of tree fell on him too. What a tragic death. They had both come down with fevers while working on the farm. They were too sick and distracted to notice the tree falling. They should've stepped to one side to avoid it, but they stepped the other way instead. They were still breathing when we tried to lift the trunk. It was terrifying. Their chins trembled violently. They bit their lips. And though their faces were bruised, there was no blood. Both were conscious and suffered until they died. Everyone was there, but nobody could do anything. In the dry season of 1965, Tầm, who didn't have enough salt in his diet and contracted malaria, died next. All the hard labor had weakened him. Then, in 1967, Hinh died. That year, we raised over one hundred pigs on the far side of the creek. But then tigers started to hunt the area for food. We fought them off, but Hinh was later killed in a forest fire.

That was the same night another tiger took our prized sow. Huy and I were so angry that we wanted to hunt and kill it. Hinh came down with a fever, so he stayed behind in the cottage. We killed the tiger the next morning and carried it back to the farm. On our return from the mountain, we were shocked to see our farm engulfed in flames. We fought off a second tiger, then took a shortcut through the bamboo forest and, without stopping, crossed a swamp to get home. Our house, kitchen, forge, bee garden—all located on the far side of the creek—were still intact. But our food storage, seeds, and pigsty had burnt to ashes. That night, the fire grew to over thirty hectares along the west bank of the Sa Thầy River. Dry leaves on the ground fed the fire. Unfortunately, it was a very windy night. For three days we searched through the debris to find Hinh's remains. He wanted to save the storehouse and the livestock, and despite his illness, he gave his life fighting the encroaching fire. After that, only Huy and I were left. At the end of 1968, during the rainy season, after six years of our living together, Huy also contracted a fever and died.

Of course, I didn't live here all by myself. Nga had been in the area for three years when Huy died. Back then, there was a road that linked B3 from Tà Xẻng to Military Base 6. The road was closed to our camp. The liaison post was located at the same waterfront where we met. The liaison people were from Bình Thuận at first, and then Nga joined the group—she is a Brigade 559 female pioneer soldier from Hải Phòng.

One day, in the early evening, while walking alone from the farm to the camp, I was surprised to see our house lit up with lanterns. I heard a guitar playing and a young woman crooning: *A soldier's life is hard . . . but to our youth, there is glory in fighting the war. . . .* I stopped at the door. The cheery scene must have been going on for a while. Huy introduced the girl: "This is Nga, a T65 liaison agent, our neighbor." She was young and tall, bewitching, and though her face showed only modesty, it was beautiful. Her skin was dark and she looked healthy, and her hair was braided in the Dutch style. She stopped singing, and I thought, what will happen to all of us now? Then she began singing again: *Days of victory, endless sorrow. . . .* Her voice crooned beautifully. Even now, returning late from the woods, I can still remember that scene and hear her songs. When I close my eyes and imagine my comrades and Nga . . .

At the end of 1967, while accompanying some guests to Ân Côc, two male T65 liaison soldiers were ambushed and killed by the Americans. The forest fire happened around the same time, destroying the T65 postal station. I invited Nga to move in and live with us in our camp. She was mad at us and refused, so she moved to the east side of the river and didn't visit us often.

I don't know whether Huy or I was more heartbroken. Probably Huy. He seemed more devastated about it than I was. He didn't play the flute often, but when he did he played it well. Soon, he started playing every afternoon, which left me in tears. Huy, by nature, was unpretentious, and he became even quieter. Now and then, I crossed the river to visit Nga and help her with chores, even though Huy never did. If Nga came by, Huy tried to avoid her. In the rainy season of 1968, Nga didn't go to Laos; instead, she was ordered to stay and look after the postal station all by herself.

When Huy died, I didn't have a chance to tell Nga, but somehow she knew about it. There was a flood that afternoon, but Nga crossed the river anyway. She went to the cemetery to visit his grave as well as the graves of my other comrades. Afterward, she came by my place and said, "I'll move in with you." Since then, the Camp of the Seven Dwarfs and the T65 postal station have merged into the same place.

We lived together in this house. I lived in the room on the right, she in the room on the left. The middle space was our living room. On days when the rain came down in sheets, I would row a boat and transport Nga and her guests across the river. However, not many people came to Military Base 6, so Nga often stayed back at camp. She did all the housework, and I did all the farm work. She was always busy with chores. Whenever I got sick, she took care of me. Sometimes, she even helped with the farming. We loved each other, but she felt lonely living here and couldn't handle the same amount of work I did. Also, the war was getting worse. After 1968, everything turned for the worse. Can you imagine that only Nga and I lived here throughout 1969? We put our harvest into storage, but nobody came to get it because all the troops had left Cánh Bắc. They had gone either to Cambodia or Cánh Nam.

I became uncivilized like Y Nua, but that doesn't make me any less human. Nga had to wear tattered clothes, which didn't cover her body completely, and this saddened her to no end. She was unhappy and felt like a forgotten prisoner. It seemed she hated me. What saddened me most was when she began to show the signs of depression that I'd experienced too. We grew distant from each other, and like me, she didn't talk for months. I didn't talk much back then. But she was different. Living like a recluse with me in the woods had done irreparable harm to her. I was fully aware of this and kept my feelings to myself. At night, I could hear Nga tossing in her hammock. Sometimes, while coming home late from the farm, I would see her standing at the gate of the camp waiting for me. When I carried home wild game, enough food to feed us for a week, or a pomelo, she seemed jovial, but this made me feel like I was deluding myself. Sometimes, I looked at her lustfully; at other times, I only gave her furtive glances. I don't know whether this was out of joy or sorrow . . .

On the first day of 1970, three scouts from the Plâyme regiment came to the camp. We didn't ask about their assignments, but we knew they were on an important mission. They were handsome and, of course, this changed the situation in Cánh Bắc. I gave them food and told Nga to take them across the river. After they reached the shore, Nga guided them toward Đắc Xiêng. The situation at B3 improved. People were sent to my camp for food. Those at the front who were responsible for logistics sent people to help me harvest my crops. Several more farms were built along the Sa Thầy River.

I still had to struggle, but my loneliness went away. At night, troops marched on the beaten paths and there was a sense of hope for the future. Nga was inspired by their youthful enthusiasm. She played the guitar and sang songs to comrades who stopped by the camp. However, her singing no longer had that spirited tone; instead, it sounded melancholic, like the sound of Huy's flute. She chose to sing the scouts' songs: *My dear soulmate, tonight is my last night seeing the moon rising over the plain.*

To me, Nga was always a compassionate person, and she became even more so. But I could sense that there was someone else between us, someone who had won her heart.

•

Mộc opened his large, calloused hands and looked at them contemplatively. He continued without looking up at me:

At the beginning of September, during the long, rainy season of 1970, a child was brought into this world. It was on a rainy night that I helped Nga deliver the baby. The task was a challenge, but fortunately both Nga and the baby turned out healthy. I took care of them.

Very few people came to the camp during the rainy months, so usually it was just the three of us. The newborn cheered up our lives. We talked more, laughed more, and argued more. Sometimes we got angry at each other because we couldn't agree on how best to care for the baby. On one unseasonably rainy night in November, I was seated at a table while Nga was in the hammock with the baby. A torch and oil lamp lit up the room. She looked at me and said, "Mộc, the baby is already two months old, and we haven't given her a name yet. I can't think of an appropriate name. Look . . ." I sat in silence for a very long time. I loved the three of us so much that it brought me to tears. We named the baby Nương.

I was thirty back then, so I thought, I'm settling down from now on and can lead a normal life, although I doubted that it was true.

I never asked Nga, and she never told me, how the baby was conceived. On the night Nương was born, I learned about Nương's father. Nga was nearly unconscious from the labor when she called out his name, begging him to be by her side. He was the commander of the group of scouts who had visited our camp. I wasn't surprised by who the father was, but I did know that the three scouts, after leaving my camp, had been killed in Đắc Xiêng after their identities were revealed. Somehow, I had the feeling that I shouldn't tell Nga the bad news, even though I didn't know at the time that she was pregnant. Because I never told her about his death, Nga's sorrow and longing for him only grew more intense. She aged quickly, and furrows appeared on her forehead. Her cheeks turned pale and sunken. I thought I should've told her the truth so that she would stop waiting for him, but I never did.

One day, a group of Ba Na ethnic conscripts came to the camp to take dried manioc to the front. They spoke in their own dialect and seemed happy because the famous Plâyme regiment had finally returned to the mountainous region. I learned this military secret by eavesdropping on them, but then I became anxious because Nga understood the Ba Na language as well.

Later that night, Nga said she would take the baby and leave me. A buzzing sound filled my ears. It seemed I couldn't hear her, but I heard every word she said. I neither yelled nor scolded her; instead, I remained calm and told her that she had to make her own decision. She wasn't officially registered here anyway, and I said to her, "Tonight or tomorrow, I'll have to go to the sugarcane farm and make sure there are no elephants," and I wished her the best. Then I left.

I returned the next morning, thinking that I hadn't properly said good-bye the night before. But she and Nương had gone. She left a letter on the table, her guitar, and the hammock. The sun had risen around six o'clock that morning, its light diffusing through the mist-enshrouded forest. I ran to the embankment and saw Nga and Nương in the middle of the river.

I called out, "Nga . . . !"

The sun, veiled by clouds, rose high above the forest. The landscape—trees, river, and water—turned a rosy color. Nga was carrying Nương on her back and stood motionless in the river. I ran toward her. It was December, during the dry season, so the water didn't quite reach my knees.

"Why are you leaving?" I pleaded to her.

She turned toward me and her AK rifle swung across the front of her chest. The water, rushing over the luminous, white sand of the riverbed, felt cold under my feet.

"Nga, please don't go!" I begged. I stopped moving toward her and asked, "What are you really looking for?"

"I already told you last night that we had to leave," she said indifferently.

"Why?" I called out. "What did I do to upset you?"

"Please don't say that." Nga shook her head. "I can't stay. Please forgive me."

"Nga," I begged again, bringing my fist to my chest, "come back with me. This has gone on long enough. Please come home."

I stood there awkwardly. Nga was silent as we looked at each other.

"Are you looking for Regiment 66?" I asked.

"Yes. I'm following the conscripted workers' footprints to get there," she replied determinedly. "I've heard he's dead, and you already knew that, but I don't believe the rumors. Mộc, listen to me, I know he's still alive."

I stood there for a while before I could say anything.

"Then why take Nương with you? Will she even survive the long journey? And what does it say about how you feel about me—by taking her with you? Why not let me take care of her? You can always come back later for her. Please, leave Nương with me because I consider her my daughter too."

"I know it's a difficult journey ahead for us, and that she might suffer along the way, but if I leave my daughter here with you, how do I know I'll ever find you again?" Nga's voice was tender, and tears swelled up in her eyes as she bowed her head.

"Where will I be? You know where I'll be. Right here, in this same forest, at this same camp, the same place where we buried our comrades. Let Nương stay with me. Listen to me, please."

I raised my arms and waded further into the river, almost buckling over into the water as I approached Nga. I snatched Nương into my trembling arms. The girl was fast asleep. I turned around and waded back through the water until I reached the shore. I looked back at Nga still standing in the river, her arms wrapped around her body. I thought there still might be another chance. Maybe Nga will come back with me and Nương, I thought. But she didn't and turned away, climbed ashore on the other side, and quickly disappeared into the hills.

Nương was like the Montagnard children who grew up on their parents' backs until they could speak and walk. The war ended. People abandoned the life of hardship and left the forest. My daughter did the same. This place belongs to the past. Nga never came back. But I stayed here, as I had promised her. This place is all I know, my battlefield, and where my comrades are buried. As for Nga, she can always come back to the Sa Thầy River and to the Camp of the Seven Dwarfs, to reunite with her daughter.

•

Mộc's weary and sun-beaten face revealed no emotion. He was quiet for a long time. Half an hour later, I stood up and we said our goodbyes. I left on the unpaved road heading in the direction of the defending post.

Giang

I was a seventeen-year-old private in Battalion 5 that year, in a company of newly recruited soldiers. Our military training took place in Bãi Nai. At the end of our three-month training camp, I earned the highest score in ballistics and thus was awarded a two-day leave. My company commander was accommodating. I didn't even have to check in on Friday night.

"You get an extra night on leave," he said, "but report back to me on time."

Hitching a ride on a military truck on Road 6, I was able to arrive home in no time at all. But for my return trip, I tried my luck with a civilian bus. Although I didn't have to report back to my unit until nine o'clock Sunday night, I still had to leave my house no later than noon to catch the bus at Kim Mã Bus Station. In those days, it was extremely difficult to get a seat on the bus, especially since it was close to Tết. Feeling reckless and yet also lucky, I found myself riding with many other passengers on the roof of the bus to Lương Sơn, where I fell off the bus and tore my sandals. My clothes got all dirty in the process.

Cold and hungry, I hobbled to a well at the town's entrance to wash off the dirt and fix my sandals. I saw someone pulling water from the well. Although it was twilight and the air was veiled by a misty rain, I could tell it was a young woman. When I approached the well, she had already filled her two tin buckets with water. She rolled up the rope and put on her conical hat, which had been placed upside down near the well. She looked ready to carry the water buckets away. My eyes quickly scanned her full name written in purple ink inside her hat: *Phạm Nhật Giang, Class 10B.* She ignored me completely and shouldered a narrow bamboo carrying pole with the buckets perfectly balanced on either side.

"Giang, please let me borrow the rope," I said, my voice sharp but composed.

She put down the bamboo pole and glanced at me. "Hello, Soldier," she said. She added after some hesitation, "Here you go."

I took the rope with my mud-stained hands.

"Oh, you're covered in filth," she said. "Here, let me help."

"Thank you, Giang. I don't want to get the rope dirty."

She pulled up one and then another bucket of water from the well. Slowly, she poured the water over my hands. I rinsed my hands carefully. As I was about to take the bucket from her, she said, "No, let me do it. It's harder than it looks to use this thing."

She dropped the rope and bucket back into the dark, seemingly bottomless well and, with amazing speed and dexterity, pulled it back up. She was extremely polite and considerate during our brief encounter. Not only did she retrieve the water for me, she also bent down and gently poured it over my calves and feet and scrubbed them until they were clean. I didn't know what to say, so I just stood there dumb, appreciating her sincerity and this unexpected act of kindness. We said nothing to each other for a long while. She even scrubbed my molded rubber sandals.

"Everything's clean now," she said.

"Nhật Giang, thank you so much."

"How do you know my name?" she asked in disbelief.

I smiled and said nothing.

"Ah, I think I know why. Just a guess, right? You soldiers are all like that. You just choose a random name, Lan, Hằng, Liên, or Oanh, and maybe you get at least one name correct."

"No," I said, "it wasn't a guess. Your name is Nhật Giang and I'm sure nobody has the same name as yours."

"Your unit must be stationed around here then."

"Not exactly. I'm stationed over in Đượm Hamlet."

"How far is that from here?" she asked.

"So, you're saying you're not from here?"

"Not at all. I'm from Hà Nội," she replied, then offered me an invitation. "I'm boarding at a place nearby. Would you like to come and rest?"

I hesitated. "I have to report back at nine o'clock tonight, and I have another ten kilometers to go."

"But it's still early. Maybe only six o'clock now."

I wanted to help Giang carry her buckets of water, but she wouldn't let me. I followed her down an unlit alley. She lived in a tiny clay-walled house with a thatch roof. There was hardly any furniture inside—only a twin bed, an American oil lamp next to a bamboo divan, a teapot and some saucers, and a ceramic bowl used for pipe smoking. A Phoenix bicycle leaned against the wall by the door. I opened the belt bag worn around my waist and took out a loaf of stale bread that my mother had given me. I poured some tea into a cup.

While fixing my sandals, Giang said, "I almost forgot there's food here. Would you like some?"

I told her it wasn't necessary, but she insisted that I wait for her to go heat up the food. While waiting, I lay down on her bed, closed my eyes, and smoked a cigarette. Then, without warning, the door was flung open and a giant of a man walked in. Startled, I sat up. He wore dark green clothes, a pair of leather shoes, and chevrons with two stripes and two stars on his sleeves, designating him as a lieutenant colonel.

"Who are you?" the man asked sternly as though it were an interrogation. "And why are you here?"

"Sir, I . . ."

At that same moment, Giang returned from the back of the house to the room with a tray of food.

"Dad, you're home," she said without missing a beat. "This is my classmate, Hùng. He's stationed not far from here. We ran into each other just now."

The lieutenant colonel's face relaxed but his stern voice remained. "Are you stationed around here?" he asked. "What unit exactly?"

"C7 K5, Company 91, sir."

"So what are you doing here at this time?"

"Sir, I was on leave. I don't have to report back until nine o'clock tonight."

"Then what's your plan—to barely make it back in time? You should return to your unit promptly."

"Dad!" Giang said. "Let him eat first. Why not sit down and join us?"

"Oh, no, but thank you," I said, feeling nervous. "Actually, I should be leaving . . ."

"It's only six kilometers from here to Đượm Hamlet," Giang's father said. He smiled. "You'll have enough time to stay and eat. Keep my daughter Giang company, since you're old friends who haven't seen each other for a while. But make sure you report back to your unit on time. Understand?" He then patted my shoulder.

"Dad, couldn't you do him a favor and call his supervisor somehow?" she insisted. "We haven't seen each other in years. There's a lot for us to catch up on."

"No," he said, shaking his head, but smiled again. "Reuniting with an old friend is a wonderful thing, but you can't keep him here all night. You don't want to see him get disciplined for violating the rules." Looking at his watch, he said, "It's already half past six. Hurry up and eat. Unfortunately, I can't join you two tonight. I have to be back at my unit as well for a meeting later. You'll be here by yourself, so make sure to lock the door."

He walked to the door and grabbed the handlebar of the bicycle on his way out. He glanced back at me and said, "Hùng, you stay and talk with Giang, but don't lose track of time."

"Will you be taking the bike with you?" Giang asked. "I was thinking I could use it to take him back to his unit later. Maybe you can walk to your unit, please? It's not that far away."

"Giang, I don't know . . ." I said, feeling even more anxious. "Maybe it isn't such a good idea . . ."

The lieutenant colonel grinned. "She's always like that, pampering her friends more than her own father. Fine, I'll walk then. No big deal. You can use the bike, since Hùng would be late if he had to walk back to his unit. Don't forget it's going to get dark outside, so be careful and don't ride too fast. After dropping Hùng off, you can take your time on the way home, but don't be back too late, because it's cold outside and I'll be worried about you."

•

That night, I rode Giang's bike with her to Bãi Nai. The streets were poorly lit and the road winding its way through the hillside was empty. I didn't feel tired although I was biking into the wind sometimes. I had never taken a girl on a bike before. A year earlier, when I was in the tenth grade, my parents bought me a bicycle, but I only used it when going around town with friends. No girl had ever sat behind me or leaned her trusting body against mine like Giang. Her Phoenix bicycle was heavy, but I barely felt its weight. We continued along a faint white line painted on the road. I pedaled up and down the sloping hills, made turns, sometimes too fast, which caused me to brake abruptly, but Giang hung steadfastly behind me. Now and then we spoke, though I let her do most of the talking. Giang had just graduated from Trưng Vương High School, and she was starting college. Her family lived in a house on Market Alley located in Khâm Thiên District. The cottage where I met her father once belonged to his friend. Giang's father had borrowed the place for her to spend Tết with him. Her mother had died last year, and her brother had left for the South a month earlier.

"Will you join us for Tết?" she asked. "Only my father and I live here, and there's nothing to do out here in the middle of nowhere. I can tell him to come pick you up where you're stationed. Then we can ask him to let us go visit Hà Nội for a few days. He loves me, so he'll agree. And if he says yes, I'm sure your boss will too."

We said goodbye at the bottom of Gừng Hill, right on the road to Đượm Hamlet, where I was stationed.

"Or I could spend Tết with you here," Giang said, letting out a sigh.

I remained on the hillside for a long time. While the dark, impenetrable night made it difficult to see this late in the year, I kept looking for her ghostly form. Now, at the moment of our separation, I was at a loss for words. I didn't even ask for her address. The only information I had was that she lived on Market Alley, Khâm Thiên District.

•

Two days later, on the 27th and just three days prior to Tết, my battalion left Bãi Nai. We marched through Thường Tín and got on a train. We didn't have a fifteen-day leave that was normally granted to soldiers who were shipping to the South. The battlefield needed more troops, and our entire division had to cross the Trường Sơn Mountains to get there. When we arrived in the Central Highlands, we joined the fighting immediately. Units of other divisions also headed to the South and were kept together. My battalion fought the first battle with my company leading the initial attack. Before the shooting commenced, the Chief of Staff visited to make sure we were all ready. He came in with an entourage of assistants and scouts, and he himself was fully armed with an automatic rifle. He wore a pair of molded rubber sandals, a Souzhou military uniform, and a combat helmet. I could still recognize him, despite how dark it was out in the woods. It was Giang's father.

I thought about running away to avoid him, but he spotted me and said, "Hey, is that you, Hùng?" He looked both surprised and happy to see me. He took my hand in his, clenching it amicably, then hugged me and said, "Giang won't stop talking about you. She's very upset she can't see you again before we leave for the South. She's now on her own."

We didn't have much time to talk since we were about to go into combat. I said nothing and only mumbled. I didn't even tell him that Hùng wasn't my name, which Giang had made up.

Before he departed, Giang's father remembered something and quipped, "Giang asked me to give you a photo of her. Unfortunately, I don't have it here with me. Hùng, next time, when we run into each other again . . . "

That "next time" never came. I didn't see Giang's father ever again, not even during the following dry season when I was ordered to go join another division. The Chief of Staff had died at the end of that previous season, right as my division joined the fray.

•

Those youthful years of my life as a soldier came and went in an instant. My memories of that time are fleeting, but they will never vanish completely, because the unexpected encounters of our lives will always remain with us, causing us great pain in the silent ways we evoke them. Maybe Nhật Giang still remembers me, just another soldier like all the nameless soldiers from thirty years ago. We met only once serendipitously, but I will never forget her, although nothing significant happened between us. I miss her, even if time has a way of drowning such memories.

Reminiscences

âm guessed that his father, usually a stern and taciturn type, wanted to talk to him about something. His family lived in a 200-square-foot room with no windows, a room with more mosquitos than natural light. Every now and then his father would comment on something, but never said more than was necessary. His father seemed disengaged from the family's daily activities. Since his retirement, he went nowhere and sat down only with his teapot at a corner table. He rarely spoke, and when he did it came off as dismissive. At night he would get up, turn off the light, and sit by himself until the next morning.

"Come over here," Tâm's father would say. "I want to . . ."

But that was all; he never completed the sentence. Since the day Tâm received his official call for enlistment, his father often repeated, "I want to tell you . . ." and Tâm would have to wait, not knowing what his father wished to say, but also not wanting to be too insistent about asking.

Then, on the fourth day of the Tết holiday just before Tâm joined the military, his father asked Tâm to accompany him on an afternoon walk. The air was humid and it threatened to rain; in fact, when the rain came it was so light that raindrops were hard to see, even though the road was wet and slippery. They strolled together without speaking. After their poor neighborhood was behind them, they entered the crowded downtown area full of meandering streets. His father often had to catch his breath while walking. The old coat he wore had several holes. Tâm held his father's elbow and helped him cross the street.

They went into an unlicensed coffee shop in the attic of an ancient, dilapidated house located next to Golden Bell Cinema. At the front, the coffee shop sold black bean sweet soup—a kind of dessert—but tucked away upstairs they served coffee. It was a creaky, chintzy attic with about five short tables and several chairs. The customers kept to themselves and appeared in silhouette; it was hard to see anyone's face clearly. The establishment had no name, but people often called it Destiny Coffee Shop.

"Once, Hà Nội was a city famous for its feminine grace, warmth, tenderness, sensitivity, but now . . ." As usual, Tâm's father didn't finish his sentence.

Their table was by a narrow window, but without a window frame it was more like a hole than a window. Through the hole, they saw the wet streets below, the attics and jagged roofs of ramshackle houses. Hà Nội, when presented this way from the back, had an odd look about it.

"This coffee shop has been around for a very long time," Tâm's father said. "It was nicer back then, but at least the coffee tastes the same. You probably didn't know this, but your grandmother used to be the proprietor of this place. On December 19, the day your grandparents evacuated, your mother decided to stay. I was sitting right here when it happened. The light suddenly fizzled out and there was gunfire. So your mother and I remained together in Interzone 1. That was our family's fate. Your mom never told you this, but she's a Catholic and I'm a Buddhist. If it wasn't for the revolution, you and your siblings would have never been born. After the revolution, we learned that our respective families had relocated to the South."

He and his father had never been close. His father showed much more affection to Tâm's younger sisters. A wall had been erected between father and son. Growing up, he felt that he had been a disappointment to his father. There were certain expectations made of him, but he couldn't figure out what they were. After he repeated the eighth grade, it was always his mother who attended the PTA meetings and signed his report cards. Once, he remembered, his father wanted to teach him French in the evenings, but then stopped the lesson after the first night and explicitly showed his disappointment. Tâm often thought his father didn't think very highly of him.

"In 1954, we were happy about you and your siblings' futures. We thought that we had traded all the hardships we'd experienced in this country for a better life for all of you. But now, with our country at war again, it's your turn to . . ."

After tomorrow, the battlefield awaited Tâm. On this afternoon, however, he sat in a corner of this coffee shop sipping his bitter coffee while listening to his father's diatribes. He sat quietly, his attention flitting from an ashtray filled with cigarette butts to his empty coffee cup. He looked at the shadows cast by other patrons huddled around tables, then leveled his eyes on the afternoon sky. It was springtime, and Hà Nội was glistening with rain.

Tâm's father ordered two more cups of coffee and pulled out a pack of Tam Đảo cigarettes from his pocket. Tâm, without hesitation, opened the pack and took out a cigarette. His father struck a match and lit it for him. Until that day, Tâm wasn't allowed to drink alcohol or coffee, and smoking was out of the question. Though his father was strict, he rarely scolded Tâm or used a rod to discipline him or any of his siblings. Once, he smacked Tâm in the face when he caught Tâm and his friends smoking at a kiosk that sold alcohol. He seemed to have forgotten that his son had already turned eighteen.

He refused to sign Tâm's application for voluntary enlistment. "Finish school. If you want to become a soldier, you must educate yourself first," he had said, not even looking at the document.

What Tâm's father didn't know or didn't want to know was that the recruitment office already knew his son very well. Although he had refused to sign Tâm's request on more than one occasion, his son remained patient. Several people who volunteered to join the military, including women, had their requests approved, but not Tâm. He was the only son in his family and was still completing high school. What he needed was his parents' signatures on the application. An officer at the recruitment office had seen Tâm multiple times and told Tâm candidly, "Right now, we don't need high school recruits who are the only sons of their families." Then, encouragingly, the recruitment officer said, "But you're very determined to go through with this. That's commendable. I wouldn't worry too much. It might take a little time, but your application will eventually be approved, because we always need people to fight the Americans."

At Tâm's age, the dejection only made him more shrewd. His legs, arms, and neck grew as puberty set in, but he felt his growth spurt was wasted. He had bad dreams at night and frequently mumbled and moaned unintelligible things from the attic. His mother fed him a bowl of herbal medicine every day, saying, "Drink this and it'll stop the nightmares."

Tâm's father didn't sign the request or even inform his wife of their son's wish to join the military. So, she believed it was Linh, who lived downstairs, who made Tâm lovesick.

Linh's family had moved to the area three years ago. She lived with her father, and they were poor. Their home was under a staircase that had been used previously as a storage room. Every day, her father, until the day he died, patiently carried a torn suitcase full of old, useless books to various street corners to sell. People didn't care to know much about his background, but they could tell he wasn't a routine street vendor. He and his daughter had lived a completely different life before. Despite their poverty, there was something quite mysterious about how they lived, which was not typical of other poor families.

Tâm and Linh were classmates but by no means friends. She was not well liked by their classmates, and Tâm tended to side with those who disliked her. For no specific reason, everybody was judgmental of her, though she tried her best to fit in. They saw in her something peculiar. Her fair complexion seemed soft, silky. Her hair and clothes were like everyone else's, but there was a kind of aloofness about her that reminded her classmates of someone from a higher social milieu.

On the first day of class, as Tâm recalled, his classmates gossiped about the perfume Linh was wearing, and how her conduct was in keeping with the bourgeoisie. She gave off a lingering scent when she walked by, but she swore in front of the class that she never used perfume or any other luxury products. "Honestly, I don't feel any different," she said as she broke down in tears. "And I can't help it even if it were true. It's just how I am . . ."

Tâm showed indifference toward Linh and distanced himself from her. Even though they lived in the same building and were in the same class, they never visited each other. When they bumped into each other in the front yard, the kitchen, at the water pump or the staircase, it was Tâm who pretended not to see her, ignoring her, and if he did have something to say, it was usually just in passing. He acted like a total stranger.

Tâm's class took a wreath to her father's funeral. Not many people attended the services, and Linh was the only immediate family member of the deceased. Tâm delivered a few shallow words of condolence to her, and nothing else. After the burial, Linh stopped coming to class and later moved out of her room beneath the staircase. Rumors said she joined the Vietnamese Youth Volunteer Organization and lived somewhere in Military Region 4,[9] or maybe in Laos. She left without saying good-bye.

9   Military Region 4 includes these provinces in the North-Central region: Thanh Hóa, Nghệ An, Hà Tĩnh, Quảng Bình, Quảng Trị, and Thừa Thiên Huế.

After Linh moved out, Tâm felt lost and empty, even though he felt their friendship never really existed. He suddenly became sentimental over her, even dreaming about her at night. In dreams from his attic, he could smell her perfume, though he knew it was only in his mind. On the other hand, his mother probably understood him better than he understood himself. She persuaded her husband to sign their son's fourth request for enlistment. Although his parents had kept their voices down, Tâm could hear their conversation from his attic room after they had woken him up that night.

"Please don't stop him," his mother said. "He wants to join the military and he loves a girl. You can't separate patriotism from romantic love, so let him go. He'll eventually find a way, regardless."

His parents signed his application. Tâm heard his mother crying to herself all night and his father comforting her. Sometimes, he heard her coughing.

The next morning, Tâm's father would accompany him to the military base. Walking on the way there, he would say to Tâm, "We want you to finish high school and go to college. You're not a real man yet, physically, and you're still immature and have lots to learn. That's why we refused to sign your application before. But now that I see how you've grown, well. . . . You're a young man living through an uncertain and dangerous time, so you can't be indifferent to the future of our country. *If you can't save your country, then you can't save your own family.* Isn't that how the proverb goes? But, son, I'm worried. I'll be fine if you decide to join the military because you realize you want to chart your own course in life, but not because you're afraid of shaming our family with a bad reputation by not going, or because you want to run away from something in your life that's making you unhappy . . ."

The wall clock struck the hour. The owner of the coffee shop turned on a light and a bulb glowed. Outside, a light rain fell, and a yellowish fog descended on the city and smothered its streetlights.

"Let's go home," Tâm's father said without standing up. "It's getting late, and you're leaving tomorrow. Tomorrow . . ."

That afternoon and evening at the coffee shop, all those days long ago, were forever embedded in Tâm's memory. Certainly, he would have chosen not to bring up these memories had it not been for his constant longing to bridge the chasm between father and son, and the sorrow of a bygone time.

Evidence

The more Minh thought about his youngest son's courageous act, the more upset Minh became. His son had almost died while trying to save someone else's life. When Minh visited me, he told me about the incident. He was so distracted by his own thoughts that he looked pathetic.

Indeed, Hùng, his son, was brave. He and his team were on a truck crossing a deserted pass in the mountainous area in western Quảng Nam. The driver, the fourth person in the truck, was reckless and, as a result, the truck flipped on its side and got lodged not quite upside-down on the road. One of the other members in Hùng's team tumbled off the side of a cliff but was saved by a tree branch. The driver was also injured, so that only left Hùng and the last squad member, who happened to be a woman, to help. Hùng himself climbed down the cliff and rescued his friend from the deep canyon.

Hùng's act of bravery was not uncommon, because many people in his situation would do the same thing. For Minh, what was hard to believe was the height of the steep cliff. According to the man Hùng saved, the distance from the truck to the bottom of the canyon was over three hundred feet. That was preposterously deep and Minh knew his son all too well: Hùng might not have a heart condition but he was deathly afraid of heights. Normally, he wouldn't dare look down due to his acrophobia. When Hùng was a kid, it had been a nightmare for him if he was anywhere near a precipice, causing him to freeze in his tracks. He couldn't even scream. When he grew up, he remained obsessed by his fear of heights. He didn't climb trees or jump off diving boards into swimming pools. He never sat on a windowsill like other boys did when they chatted. As a grown-up, he would sweat and close his eyes when he saw someone parachuting out of an airplane on TV. Even now, it was a tormenting experience when he boarded an airplane. He would quietly struggle to keep his composure so that he wouldn't look too panicked to other passengers.

Hùng didn't tell his father about his courageous act. Minh only learned about it from the man his son rescued, who stopped by the house with his parents to thank Hùng. Minh talked with his son the following day, warning him about the risks, but also praising him for his unselfish act. But Hùng shook his head, explaining that what made him do it was not that his friend might die; rather, it had to do with the cliff itself. His explanation didn't make much sense, but Minh realized that the accident offered his son an unexpected opportunity: after so many years Hùng was finally able to overcome his fear of heights while rescuing his friend.

"Hùng has always surprised me since he was a kid," Minh said in a wistful voice, turning the wineglass in his hand. "But I am worried by what he just did. At first his action shocked me, and now it troubles me unbearably. I've been feeling this way for several days."

"Have you lost your mind?" I laughed, looking at Minh. "You should be proud of him instead. You look disheartened as if your son had done something evil."

"Well, I know that. But that's not what I meant." Minh went on, trying to explain: "I mean, I'm troubled because my son isn't like me at all. He's completely different. . . . When people told me about how he saved his friend, I asked myself, when I was his age, would I have acted the same way? Well, I suppose so, since I used to save people's lives, too. . . . You saw it—on the Mễ Sở boat—remember? An elderly woman fell off the boat into the water and I immediately jumped in to rescue her. I was the only one to do it—not you or any of our friends. I'm not saying that makes me a hero and the rest of you cowards. I'm an excellent swimmer and knew that I was able to help the woman easily. On the other hand, you guys don't swim very well and could've died trying to save her. So, what I'm trying to say is that what I did back then is completely different from what my son did. He's nothing like me. What does it mean? Who did he inherit his courage from?"

I laughed and was somewhat surprised. "Listen to you! You're his father, so why do you think so poorly of him? As they say, *like father, like son*—you can't argue with that, but it's not uncommon for you and your son to have a different temperament."

"The way my son is—he keeps to himself and doesn't take risks," Minh said. "Nobody knows that except me. When he was a little boy, he rarely showed emotion—he didn't express joy or sorrow. My parents thought he was headstrong as a child, but I knew he wasn't. When he got startled from sleep he would pee himself. He used to stop himself from crying by grinding his teeth. Later, as a student, he was known for being stubborn. He always kept his head lowered and didn't greet adults or teachers. He spoke softly. People assumed he was rude but also confident. But that's not true—he was shy and acquiesced to others. I loved him but was annoyed by this behavior, especially because I wouldn't have acted like that at all. Although he kept to himself, he often got into fights with his classmates and the other kids in town. Once, a group of hoodlums gathered at the gate to his school. All of Hùng's friends got scared and gave the thugs whatever they had in their pockets. My son resisted and the bullies beat him up. When I heard about this, I gave him advice, but he didn't want to listen to me, so I had to transfer him to another school. I was a student myself once, but I wasn't so timid, and I knew some martial arts I'd learned from my oldest brother. But I never got into fights—if people leave me alone, then I leave them alone."

Normally, Minh didn't stay long when he visited me, and he refused to drink wine when I offered. But if he did have thoughts to share, then he drank himself into a stupor and wouldn't shut up. He told me a story:

"When Hùng was ten, I took him for a walk. He wanted ice cream, so I bought it for him. He stood on the Tràng Tiền sidewalk, an ice cream cone in his hand, and just as he was about to eat it, a bully snatched it from him. My son stood there and didn't know what to do. That was the first time he encountered such a thing. I felt sorry for him and held his hand, saying, "It's okay, son. Don't worry about it. I'll buy you another one." Before I finished my sentence, he jerked his hand away from mine and started chasing the other kid. I yelled and ran after him, but I lost sight of him in the chaos of traffic. You can imagine how scared I was. When I arrived at Ngô Quyền District, I saw him emerging from an alleyway. He was holding the ice cream's bamboo stick. There was still some ice cream, a green color, left on the stick. I had never scolded my son until that moment, but I grabbed him, reproached him, and spanked him. I was still angry when we got home. That was the first time my wife and I had a heated argument and the first time I questioned Lan harshly about *her* son. Ever since then, a terrible and irrational thought has been nagging at me. And now, I feel even more skeptical after Hùng's recent courageous act."

I was about to ask Minh what he was skeptical about. And then I understood what he had on his mind.

Minh, Lan, and I were classmates who lived in the same town. To Lan, Minh and I were just friends. After high school, I joined the military, Lan went to Russia, and Minh ended up in Germany. We reunited after the war ended, but I didn't see any difference in the way Lan treated Minh. I was only somewhat surprised when I received their wedding invitation, because I always thought they were a good match. I knew that Minh had adored Lan since high school, and he'd waited for her patiently since then, hoping that his love for her might be reciprocated. That she agreed to marry him seemed like the right decision.

Even now, I think Minh and Lan are just like many other couples. They get along, live rather happily, and have led a decent life. Of course they argue over things, just like anybody else, even if nobody outside their family knew.

Their oldest daughters are twins and this, for several years, was the root of Minh's unhappiness. When Lan gave birth to a son, Minh was elated, a feeling common among new fathers. For years afterward he liked telling people how much his son looked like him, which was true. From the age of eleven to twenty, Hùng looked exactly like Minh when he was younger. So why was it necessary for Minh to emphasize their resemblance so proudly? Back then, I was amused by Minh's boasting but didn't pay too much attention to it. Now, I think I understand.

Minh and I have been friends for many years, but my former friendship with his wife is never mentioned. All I know is that Lan is now his spouse, and I try to forget any story associated with her in the past.

In those days, there were four of us: Minh, Lan, Tuấn, and myself. That's it! Hùng's temperament, the way his father describes it, is exactly like Tuấn's.

Tuấn's parents were high-ranking state officials. Because he was their only son, they pampered him so much that he became inarticulate and got scared easily. Only his friends understood his timid behavior. At school and around the neighborhood, Tuấn always got into fights. He was fearful of his teachers but had a reputation for being disobedient. Being born into a wealthy family made him awkward and self-conscious, although he won all the games other poorer children played.

I didn't know whether Tuấn really had a fear of heights, but I was certain that he feared loud explosions. As a kid and as a teenager, he would go around town with other neighborhood children during the

Tết holidays, and hearing firecrackers always terrified him. He tried his best to put on a good face and didn't cover his ears or hide in his house. He handled the firecrackers with the rest of us, but I could tell he was scared. Afterward, he became a soldier and fought for a few years, but his fear of loud explosions never went away. That was who he was, but he also turned out to be a brilliant and skillful B41 gunner.

Tuấn and I joined the military at the same time. He was the only son of his family, so enlistment wasn't mandatory for him, but he nevertheless made his parents and the local recruitment office approve his application for enlistment. He wanted to wear a soldier's uniform. I tried to discourage him from joining the military, knowing that he didn't have the physical strength and was too timid. Once, he almost beat me up for trying to stop him. But he was afraid of loud noises, the sight of blood, rats, snakes, and so on. We were in the same squad of new recruits. Tuấn was an indulged son of a well-to-do family and for the first time in his life he had to experience adversity. I loved him but couldn't help him, because he would get mad if anyone offered him assistance. On our way to the South, I quietly observed how he struggled with himself as we crossed rivers and mountains, or at times when we retreated from artillery strikes.

When we arrived at B3, Tuấn and I were transferred to the same company. He matured into his role more quickly than I did and eventually got promoted after only two dry seasons. I wasn't surprised. In our battalion, everybody complimented him on his intelligence, perceptiveness, enthusiasm, and especially his camaraderie in how he treated his other fellow soldiers. However, this didn't square with what I knew about him, because Tuấn was still the same Tuấn I had always known.

After the 1972 campaign, Tuấn studied for six months at the Front Military Academy, then returned to his old unit and became the company's lieutenant commander. I was a sergeant and the interim political instructor at the time. We worked side by side. After our first battle, Tuấn came back to his unit and displayed an aptitude for leadership and superb knowledge about the war. He was calm, firm, decisive, and the way he was versed about the situation showed his intelligence. However, I was his close friend and knew him well. Beneath it all, he was still fearful and timid, and he struggled with this innate weakness. A bomb suddenly exploding would startle us, but for Tuấn he would become extremely nervous and freeze up. If he saw submachine guns firing over his head, he tried his best to be strong, but nobody knew this about him except for me. In fact, that was how I felt about Tuấn, because he hid his fear and never showed it openly.

I was sometimes amused by Tuấn's behavior, but deep down in my gut, I loved and even admired him. We both faced difficult events in our lives, and while I wasn't as fearful, Tuấn struggled with the deep psychological effects of war more than anyone else I knew, including myself.

When Tuấn became the company commander, it was in the period after the Geneva Accords. We had plenty of food and weapons. We also received lots of letters. Whenever my company received parcels, Tuấn got a letter sent to him by Lan from Eastern Germany. She sometimes wrote to me, too, because she knew that Tuấn and I were in the same unit. Even though the letters were addressed to me, they contained the passionate language of her love for Tuấn. They had been secretly in love for a long time, though it wasn't until Tuấn said goodbye and left to become a soldier, and not until after Lan had gone abroad, that they expressed their love for each other.

After Tuấn died, Lan's letters to him were still delivered to the company regularly. I put all of her unopened letters into his rucksack. It was thick with correspondence. However, everything about Tuấn's life and struggles had nothing to do with Minh's married life. How could Minh have such an irrational doubt about Hùng, his son born after so many years, when Lan's first love was already over? Probably there was some kind of inexplicable connection between the son and the man whom Lan had loved, although he had died a long time ago.

Minh didn't know how to explain this unrealistic connection, but he had evidence to prove his assumptions. For example, when Hùng, Lan's awkward son, tried to control his innate phobias and risked his life to rescue his friend off that steep cliff, was this the evidence Minh was looking for?

The Secret of the River

Rivers, like time, flow. Countless events in life are marked this way, by the flow of time and on the waters of the rivers. This is especially true at night when specks of light inexplicably appear on the waters of my hometown's river, a river that contains the secret of my life.

Once upon a time, beneath a full moon at the height of the flood season, American bombs rained on the dikes of my village. In mid-July of the lunar year, the bombers unleashed their payloads onto our rice paddies.

Earlier that same afternoon, I had been informed that my wife was in labor, but I was not permitted to leave my workstation at the dike. Later, after the dike broke, all I could think about was our baby. I hurried back to my village as fast as I could to head off the oncoming flood, even as the floodwaters nipped at my heels. I saw my village entirely swamped. I made it home, but as soon as I helped my wife successfully onto the thatched roof of our house, the water crested and carried it away. By some miracle, just when it was about to break apart, the roof hit an enormous banyan tree and lodged itself next to the village's communal house. A huge crowd had sought safety on the tree's branches, and many of them extended their arms to help lift my family up. My wife, clutching our newborn tightly, refused to let me help her.

"It's a boy, it's a boy," she kept saying. "You have nothing to be frightened about, my son." Then she said to me, "No, let me keep him. You're too clumsy."

Several hours passed. The downpour intensified as gusts blew in and the sky opened up into a raging tempest. Even after the floodwaters stopped rising, the current remained too swift, forcing more and more people to take sanctuary in the banyan tree. I was consumed by exhaustion. My wife, chilled to the bone and soaking wet, started to lose her strength in the water. I clutched her with determination and used my free arm to cling to the tree's V-shaped trunk.

By the next morning, after having saved my wife, we heard a watery splash beneath the tree branch we were both perched on.

"Please save us! Save my daughter!" a woman cried out.

A cold, ghostly hand covered in muck brushed against my legs. I quickly bent down and probed the water with my hands. But the woman's hand slipped away and disappeared beneath the surface. Suddenly, our tree's branch shook violently and snapped. My wife screamed in horror, "Oh, no!" A plopping sound followed. My newborn son, whose face I still had not yet seen clearly, fell from the elastic satchel in my wife's arms and was carried under the murky waters.

"Oh, my God!" she shrieked. "My son!"

Immediately, she dove into the water after him. I followed my wife into the freezing water, which was murky and bottomless. I was able to wrestle my son away from the strong current and quickly lifted him up to others who were reaching out to help. Then I plunged back into the swift current to rescue my wife. Other villagers also jumped in to help me.

Later, when I regained consciousness, the sun had risen and the rain had abated. I was sprawled out against the hull of a rescue dinghy surrounded by people. I had struggled frantically against the vengeful, perilous tide the night before and failed. Blood was pouring from my ears and nose. I could not find my wife, or any sign of her. When the patrol boat arrived, I was pulled forcibly out of the water. Drained of energy, I fainted. After some more time passed, I woke up feeling terribly sore. My tears were hot like fire.

A woman came up and tried to comfort me, saying, "I'm sorry about what happened to your wife, but you must stay strong to raise your child. Thank Heavens you were able to save the baby! For a newborn to have to experience such a horrific event! But look at him now. He's doing just fine. Someone just breastfed him earlier. He's asleep now. What a sweet, sweet boy."

"He's soiling himself," I said.

While the woman began to caress my child, she slowly unwrapped the blanket that had kept him warm. She started to change my son's diaper. I looked down at him and felt overwhelmed with astonishment, saying aloud, "My child, my child!" I wept and cradled the blanketed newborn in my arms.

Several years after these events, and having myself ripened into old age, my daughter became the most beautiful girl in our village. She was indeed a daughter of the river, as it was said, because I had rescued her from its floodwaters. Everybody thought they knew the truth. But there was a secret that no one, not even my daughter, knew. Only the river kept its secret: day after day I would go down to the rebuilt dike to watch the waters of the river flow. My wife, my son, and the unnamed woman gazed at me from the depths of the river.

Time may be fleeting, and even as the river, like history, flows forever onward, I am still haunted by the deep, unspeakable sorrow of this chapter in my life.

An Unnamed Star

The moon looms overhead as our train stops at Phúc Trạch Station. Ten minutes later we start up again, groaning through the hilly backcountry, the lowlands, and across this immense and godforsaken stretch of western Quảng Bình Province. A section of the Trường Sơn Mountains crosses through here, a desolate region full of reeds and undergrowth stretching as far as the eye can see. Soon, our train enters the black tunnel of a mountain and emerges on the other side into a moonlit expanse.

"Look there," a woman sitting at the other end of the car points out. "It's the 500 kV electric power line."

Until now, I thought I was the only passenger in the car to be up this late. The train lurches from side to side, its iron wheels grinding violently as it barrels down the tracks. A soft wind wanders through the cabin, lulling people to sleep. Outside the window, the moon appears luminous, the landscape blurring into the long night ahead. Signal poles. Railroad switches. Underbrush and trees. Sloping hilltops. A ribbon-like forest. I hear clanging as we cross a small, rickety bridge. In this lonely wasteland, my country stretches into the infinite.

•

Thirty years have now passed and much about the world has changed. Although events from the past may diverge from the present in profound ways, the mountains, the forests, the rivers and their tributaries remain the same. Quảng Bình still has its distinctive terrain: a strip of land, the immeasurably wide Trường Sơn Mountains, and the sky that stretches into an infinite expanse. Besides the newly constructed 500 kV power line that runs from the North to the South, two decades of peace have stamped on this pathetically bleak terrain only a railroad. Progress and change have happened elsewhere in the country, but somehow never made it here. The war against time ends when the train's whistle stops hissing, and the hands of the clock move only when a train passes through. Only their coming and going signal the days and nights.

Back in my youth, during my generation, soldiers who left Hà Nội and went South were considered very lucky if they went by train, even if that meant getting off at the stop in northern Cầu Bùng where the railroad ended. From Quỳnh Lưu, men slung weapons over their shoulders and walked through Nghệ An, Hà Tĩnh, the Ngang Pass. Then they either made a beeline to Cự Nắm or would take the road to Troóc. The liaison road 559, thousands of miles long, started there and went all the way to the South. In the winter one year, I remember my battalion marching through Khe Gương. Infantrymen waded through an area where there was once a bridge. The bridge had collapsed and fallen into the ravine a long time ago, and only its abutment remained. What was left of the burnt structure lay in ruins from neglect, but it still stood spectacular, emerging from the deep gorge like the arch of an ancient citadel, or a wrecked boat left marooned there in the canyon. Chunks of the bridge's platform swathed in thick moss lay scattered below among white pebbles in the cold, glassy water.

I remember when I was seventeen, before the collapse of this remarkable bridge, the feeling of being awestruck by its grandeur, and wondering why anyone would invest in building such a structure in the desolate mountains. Even more surprising, that they had built this bridge for the train. I was born into an urban family, to parents who were state officials, but besides the little I gleaned from history books I knew almost nothing about my country's past. I used to think that the North–South train traveled only from Hà Nội to Vinh, so how is it that there is a railway bridge in Quảng Bình?

"The bridge didn't collapse because of the enemy's artillery fire," my battalion commander had told me back then, "but because of our Việt Minh troop's scorched-earth policy."[10]

In those days, on the other side of the canyon, we had marched along a railroad, although the remnants of the railroad were gone by then— no tracks, no ties, no gravel to provide stability. The passage of time, the trees and vegetation, and erosion had reclaimed this North–South railway, turning it into a nameless, beaten path along the steep hills.

The uneven road meandered through the fog-enshrouded land. My battalion had turned into Rú Vọc and would set up camp there for a few days. Out here in the scrubby hinterlands, we were ordered not to sleep in our hammocks at night. Instead, we had to dig trenches and build shelters because it was Tết, so that we could properly celebrate the New Year.

Each squad was allotted their own shelter. We dug A-shaped trenches and built Hoàng Cầm stoves[11] to dissipate the smoke and avoid enemy detection; we made makeshift beds, racks for our guns and rucksacks, and set up an altar where we hung our national flag and a photograph of Hồ Chí Minh.

---

10 "A military strategy of burning or destroying crops or other resources that might be of use to an invading enemy force." (oxfordreference.com)

11 "The Hoàng Cầm stove, named after its inventor, a Viet Minh soldier in 1951, was a stove intake and chimney system which diffused and dissipated smoke from cooking which prevented aerial detection of smoke by American military planes. They were used extensively in the Củ Chi tunnels and other hideouts." (http://www.owlapps.net)

"Everything looks good," said Tỏ, the squad leader. "As good as the barracks for non-commissioned officers anyway. But we can't just eat military rations for New Year's Eve. That's ridiculous."

Tỏ had served in the military for two years, so he knew the lay of the land. It didn't take him long to realize that in this isolated forest, remote as it was, there had once been a logging camp. So he reasoned that there had to be people living nearby, most likely a small settlement of woodsmen somewhere close. Tỏ opened a sack and all of us scrounged through our rucksacks for items we could give him to barter for food ahead of celebrating Tết: sewing supplies, firestones, Văn Điển batteries, Golden Star balm, razors, hairpins, dehydrated rations, canned meat, sugar, and milk. Tỏ requested that I go with him.

At first, we followed the arc of the horizon. Eventually Tỏ found an old footpath hidden in the thorny underbrush. We walked on the abandoned path for over an hour and, arriving at a skeletal forest, we stumbled on a railroad. Unlike the railway in Khe Gương, the tracks in Rú Vọc, although partly obscured by reedy patches, remained visible, emerging before us like a bulwark against the surging tide.

We weren't sure which direction to go, but then through the cold mist we spied a cottage at a bend in the tracks. We pushed the reeds aside and walked toward it. Upon closer inspection, it didn't look like a cottage at all; it looked, rather, like a signalman's elevated platform. The structure had collapsed and was completely ruined. I parted a torn mat that was used as a door to the cottage and noticed a man, far past his prime, sitting on a stool. He had a hunched back and his furrowed forehead looked like the skin of a dry apple. His lower jaw sagged, probably because he had lost most of his teeth. He was wearing an oversized fur-lined coat with small, colorful patches, though most of the fur had fallen off.

"Hello, sir," I said.

"What the hell do you want?" he barked.

"Why are you sitting here in the cold?" I asked.

"Well, ain't that a dumb question," the old man said, irritated. "You blind? Can't you see what I'm doing here? You Northern folk are always griping about something."

"Is there a village nearby, sir?" Tỏ asked.

The old man couldn't stop coughing. I repeated Tỏ's question, only enunciating more clearly.

"What do you want with me?" the old man said.

"Sir, we just want to trade a few things—like MREs for fresh food, so that both soldiers and civilians can celebrate Tết," Tỏ answered.

The old man struggled to get on his feet. He took a raincoat made from dry leaves off the wall and hobbled outside. Standing in his mud-caked shoes, he pointed in the direction of the forest. "Over there," he said. "The town's over there. There's also a logging camp. A school. Even an arboretum—"

"Excuse me, sir," I interrupted, "did you say there's a town?"

"You think only the North has towns?" he said, raising his voice. "Go past the arboretum and creek, then swing right. Keep heading straight, then take another right. Go straight again past the hill. See that hill yonder? The logging camp you're looking for is on the other side. You can find food there."

The old man gave confusing directions. His accent was not typical for Quảng Bình.

"Do you live there?" Tỏ asked.

"Another stupid question!" the old man barked. "Why would I live with the woodsmen?"

"Then why are you sitting here?"

"I'm a signalman."

I was dumbfounded. Then I saw the brass whistle swinging around his neck. Clutched in his fists were two small flags—one yellow, the other red.

"Let me tell you, the woodsmen living there have it rough. Don't think you can trade anything with them. But that's the only town in Rú Vọoc."

"Where do you live then, sir?" I asked.

"At the train station."

"The train station? Where's that?"

The old man raised his graying eyebrows and looked at me with his wide, cloudy eyes. He seemed genuinely surprised by my ignorance. Then he pivoted around slowly.

"Over there is the train station," he said, pointing toward an emerald forest beyond where the railroad tracks curved away. "Come over to my place when you come back. I want to buy some things from you, too. I have money, you know. But because there's nobody here, there's nothing ever to buy even if you have money. Do you have patterned fabric?"

"No, we don't," Tỏ said.

"How about scented soap?"

"Not that either."

"What about mirrors—things women like?"

"Again, no. Do you really need all that stuff?"

"No, but I want to buy them for Mai, my granddaughter. Hey, so whatcha got in that bag? Don't be shy. I'll buy whatever you got. I have money, you know."

As I started to answer the old man's question, Tỏ hushed me with his hand. He thanked the old stranger and pulled me aside. "Can't you see the old guy's batshit crazy?" he said, reprimanding me. "Don't be a fool. He has nothing to trade. Don't tell him what we have or he'll find a way to rob us."

Regardless, we followed the directions Crazy Grandpa had given us and headed toward the logging camp and town. We crossed a new-growth forest that had once been decimated by B-52 bombers. The bombardment happened a long time ago, and now buds were sprouting in places on the fallen, scorched trunks. Through the dead vegetation, we could still make out remnants of houses. Shattered bricks and bomb craters, along with caved-in roofs and floors, dotted the area. The wind picked up.

"There's the town," Tỏ said. "Crazy Grandpa sure is funny."

Finally, we arrived at the logging camp. What used to be a forest had been completely flattened by bombing. The paths were hidden by wild foliage, causing a rustling sound as the dry, broken branches snapped beneath our feet. We didn't see anyone else along the way, but there were signs of human life: a scattering of cottages, or what remained of them anyway, and other buildings half-buried in the earth.

"It looks like they closed the market here early for Tết," Tỏ said sarcastically.

From our periphery, a group of children emerged from the bushes. Their clothes barely clung onto their bodies. They had mottled skin and looked emaciated, beyond sickly. Their lips were tinted blue, most likely due to the cold climate.

"Hey, you guys!" the kids called out to each other, jumping up and down excitedly. They approached us. "Maybe these soldiers want to trade their razors for our chickens."

"Where are your families?" I asked.

"My dad works for the railroad," a kid answered. "My mom's in Cổn to buy some salt."

"My parents are planting corn," another kid said.

"What's in your bag?" the apparent leader of the group asked. "Do you want to trade your army rations for our chickens or what?"

"Sure," I said. "We need fresh food. Do you have any at home?"

"Knock it off," Tỏ grumbled. He frowned and muttered at me, "There's nothing for us to trade here. Can't you see their condition? Let's give each household something instead—some small gifts from us soldiers to the civilians for Tết."

We visited thirteen homes in the backwoods village. The kids tagged along with us. At each entrenchment we opened our rucksack and placed a few items into a combat helmet as an offering. Gathering around us, the kids could hardly contain their excitement. We went into the half-buried bunker homes and greeted the people living there. Even though each household had a stove, the dwellings were otherwise spartan and unlit, and very cold. In each home we met either an elderly man or woman. Putting the items in a helmet on the mat, I said, "The new year isn't here yet. My comrades and I are just passing through so we can't stay long, but we'd like to give your family some small gifts and wish you a Happy New Year."

Some of the more elderly residents thanked us. Others just blinked, staring blankly at us with their sunless eyes.

Tỏ and I returned on the worn path. We walked, each in our own thoughts, and each feeling very despondent. It was around noon and the rain had stopped. The air, however, remained chilly. The forest unfurling before us seemed vaster, more dreary. A sea of reeds appeared the color of ash. Aircraft rumbled in the sky overhead.

We continued down the tracks toward the signalman's wooden cottage. He was standing dutifully outside his cottage, facing north, where several planes with thunderous engines were idling in the distance. He extended one of his hands.

"What's he doing?" I asked curiously.

"Can't you see he's holding a flag?" Tỏ answered. "It's a yellow flag to announce an oncoming train. Maybe he thinks the aircrafts' rumbling is the sound of a train coming in?"

The old man didn't pay attention to us when we approached him. He kept his eyes trained on the railroad tracks, holding out his arm without the slightest hint of fatigue. The yellow flag flapped in the wind. I was about to greet the old man, but Tỏ hushed me again. We hid in the cane grass and circled away from him. When we were a good distance from him, Tỏ said, "We have to avoid him because I realized we didn't give him anything."

We kept to ourselves the rest of the way back. When we almost reached our squad's encampment, Tỏ told me to stop for a second by a creek.

"I feel sorry for Crazy Grandpa," Tỏ said, "but I can't leave the platoon again, so you'll have to go back by yourself. You can rest up for a bit, then head back to his cottage with gifts for Tết. I can even get the gifts ready for you. I have everything he wants—patterned fabric, scented soap, and all the things girls like—sewing kits, hairpins, buttons. I don't have a round mirror, but Ngữ in A2 has one, so I'll ask him to give it to the crazy guy's granddaughter. Will you go to him, please? If you hurry, you'll make it back in time for New Year's Eve before you know it."

"Sure," I said.

•

I devoured my rations and didn't rest. Afterward, I grabbed my rucksack and set off immediately. A cold, misty rain fell that afternoon, and when I arrived at the cottage the old man was nowhere to be found. What was left of the railroad tracks seemed to add to the site's bleakness. The place was quiet, only the hills and the endless mountains stretched into the wet horizon. Feeling completely exhausted, I dragged my feet along the bend in the battered tracks and continued toward the new-growth forest where the train station, according to the old man, was located. I had thought he was senile with his incoherent muttering, but there was, in fact, the remains of a train station. This was the first time south of Vinh that I'd seen rusted tracks and railroad ties covered by grass. On this parcel of unbroken land, among the jagged rocks, appeared a long-forgotten railway platform. A path wound into a thicket of newly planted trees, and thinking this was part of the depot's construction, I followed it into the forest.

In the forest, a house emerged unexpectedly in the afternoon's drizzle. The house didn't have a tile roof or even a thatched one; it was neither a cottage nor one of those half-buried bunker dwellings. Although the structure was almost completely covered in vines, I was surprised when I realized that it was a train car. The car sat on tracks buried in the ground and overgrown with vegetation. Some loofah sponges were hanging in the front windows. The car had doors on either end. The original steps were broken and had been replaced by makeshift wooden planks. The brass handrails, however, still looked genuine.

I hesitated as I stopped in front of the door. For what seemed like a long time, I just stood there silently. Then, behind my shoulder, I felt a presence. The figure, like a ghost, had crept up on me without making a sound. I turned to face it. In the evening's dying light, I saw its profile very clearly, a face not of a ghost but one belonging to a young woman. Her unearthly features would be burned into my memory for a long time after, reappearing to me in the shadowy light of an altar.

"Good evening, comrade," the young woman said. Her voice was soft and melodic. "Are you looking for my grandfather?"

"Are you Mai?" I asked.

"Yes," she said softly, nodding, and invited me into her "house."

The wooden floors creaked under my weight as I entered. The train car smelled like burning joss, which I imagined was on an altar somewhere in the dark but couldn't see. Mai and I sat down on a wooden bench. I knew it was a third-class passenger car because only two long benches stretched beneath the windows. The old signal-man, coughing as he struggled to breathe, was lying down on the opposite bench.

"Why doesn't he have a bed?" I asked.

"He likes it that way. He's used to it by now. He's been sleeping on the bench like that for years."

"Just you and your grandfather live here?"

"Yes. There used to be more people living here—my parents and younger siblings."

"You should light that lamp," I said after a moment of silence. "President Johnson announced there won't be bombings during Tết. I haven't seen aircraft since this afternoon."

"You're right. I heard the same thing. But my grandfather is afraid of the light at night. If he's asleep, he gets up, terrified that somebody struck a match, or flicked a lighter. He'd run away. My grandfather, you see, he's senile—but you probably already know that. Did you meet him at the railroad earlier?"

I told Mai how Tỏ and I had met her grandfather, and why I came back.

"Well, that's him for sure," Mai sighed. "When he was much younger, a French train used to run through here. Back then, he had arrived here from Huế to become a signalman. He told me that this was used as a ranger station, also called Mả Phu Tàu Station.[12] The name sounds scary, doesn't it?"

"What about this train car?" I asked. "How long has it been here?"

"Long before I was around. Actually, I was born right here in this car seventeen years ago. My parents told me this passenger car belonged to the last North–South train that passed through here. The train transported people evacuating from Huế to Vinh. There was never enough coal, so it chugged along slowly. When the French attacked Đồng Hới, they had to unhitch this car so the rest of the train could move faster. After the attack, no more trains came through here. People blew up bridges and railroads everywhere to protest the French. My grandparents and parents pushed this train car along the crossing loop and hid it in the forest. They lived here for nine years during the revolution. Then the French bombed the station, and my family has lived here in this car since."

"Why live in such a remote place for so long?"

"My grandmother died here," Mai said. "My grandfather doesn't want to live too far from where she's buried. Anyway, he tells me his life is part of the train station and the railroad. He believes that one day the trains will run again. Even though peace has already been restored, year after year he doesn't want us to relocate. So he lives here awaiting his train. Because of that, my parents decided to stay here as well, and they went to work at the logging camp. Rú Voọc

---

12   Mả Phu Tàu literally means *the graves of railroad coolies*.

wasn't always deserted like this. During less turbulent years, the town was full of people. We had a logging camp, a ranger station, several blacksmiths, and wood shops. There was also a market in town, an elementary school, and a middle school. My parents even invited my grandfather to live with them in a tiled house in town, but after only a few days, the Americans bombed us and destroyed everything. Many people lost their lives, my parents, too, when the bombs fell on the logging camp. After that, I took my grandfather and siblings to Military Zone 4, and we lived in one of those half-buried bunkers. Last winter, my younger brothers got up and built a fire to keep themselves warm. A plane saw the campfire and launched its rockets. The missile hit the door of our bunker and killed both my brothers at the same time. I was wounded and my grandfather lost his memory of the attack. After that, he returned to the boxcar and now lives here. I live with him and take care of him. He doesn't count the days. He has no idea what month it is; he can't even tell the holidays apart. Every day, he walks to the cottage to welcome an approaching train. He sleeps here at night and refuses to sleep in a bunker. It's not aircraft that he's afraid of, but the light."

I sat quietly near Mai and listened to her story. She talked without stopping. I could only imagine how she felt, how the loneliness must be gnawing at her heart. She hoped one day to see a real train arriving, just to see what it would look like; to hear the sound of its iron wheels trembling along the tracks, to hear its whistle. But she had never seen a real train, so it was difficult for her to imagine.

"When they bring back the railway, the trains will bellow through here again," Mai said, her voice imbued with hope, "and my grandfather will regain his memory." Then she added jokingly, "We'll connect this car back to the train and sit in our 'house' as it travels around the country."

•

The dark night descended on New Year's Eve. The rain had let up and stars freckled the sky, making it look somewhat clearer. We said goodbye at the mouth of the forest, and Mai pointed at a brilliant blue star in the northern sky.

"Do you know the name of that star?" she asked.

"No," I said. "I'm guessing it doesn't have a name. Probably because we already have the Great Bear, which is much bigger and more brilliant, to indicate which direction is north."

"My grandfather says that in the past, when that star appeared overhead, above the mountaintops, it meant the North–South train was approaching."

I told Mai that my squad and I would return to her house the following morning, the first day of Tết, to wish them a Happy New Year. I added while clasping her soft hands in mine, "We'll help you push the car and make it run again."

At three o' clock in the middle of the night, we were given new orders to march. We would immediately march toward the west, leaving the railroad behind.

•

Now, thirty years have passed. No one on the train's crew tonight knows about Mả Phu Tàu Station, probably because they don't know where all the railroad switches are located. My eyes stay focused on the moonlit night. Outside the windows, the mountains flash by, coming and going in an endless chain. Tonight, as I look out, I see a blue star above the mountain ridge chasing our train. Names of places flicker through my mind, but they escape my imagination before I can commit them to memory, as though the names themselves are snatched away by the wind.

Hà Nội at Midnight

L ast year, many people in my company had their houses built. The contractors tried their best to finish the construction in a timely fashion, so that new tenants could move in prior to Tết. For the tenants, moving into new homes with high ceilings, spacious rooms, and walls that separated their estates from the outside world meant embracing the modern age. But for me, no longer a young man, I was left with only reminders of a bygone era.

As typical for this time of year, it was humid but sunny for the entire month. According to the lunar calendar, there were only twenty-nine days in December. Nhật Tân cherry blossoms were blooming and a northeasterly wind had blown in prior to the day the Kitchen God went to Heaven. The weather would remain frigid until the next full moon. For the past several years, as many people recalled, the last cold snap had been during the Tết holiday of the Year of the Dragon 1964 and didn't happen again until the Year of the Tiger 1998.

By some fortune, the new house I moved into was in the same neighborhood as the house where I spent my childhood. The old house was No. 4, and my current house is No. 102, located on opposite ends of the street. During my first Tết in the new house, the weather was reminiscent of the time I had spent Tết in the old one. Because I found myself associating more with that previous era, I felt like I hadn't changed much even if my living situation did. I couldn't sleep, I drank too much, I lost track of time. My mind often wandered. I wasn't home much during the day, and I also went out at night.

This town, populated with trees in my youth, extended far into the distance. I remembered hearing the trolley bell as I watched it blaze through an intersection. Now, standing on the roof of a three-story house, I couldn't see past the wall of the house next door. Back in those days, there were no houses in this part of town—only wide-open spaces for weeds to grow and for ghosts to wander. Now the land was gone, and in its place appeared tall buildings of concrete and tin-roofed tenements with glass windows. This was inevitable, perhaps. Thirty-four years had passed. Not too long ago, they made a documentary series about Hà Nội at the beginning of the Reform period,[13] and the director, a distinguished artist, had taken his crew to a town in Bắc Ninh to make the film. The Hà Nội of the film, although inspired by the real setting, didn't look quite like Hà Nội. The prewar spring of the Year of the Dragon 1964 had escaped everyone's memory. No longing for that earlier time could bring it back. But someone strolling at night today, leaving the real world comfortably behind, could still escape into the old world. Crossing one side of the street into another, from the present to the past, was like traveling back through time. The Hà Nội of that earlier spring still lingered in the air and returned to mingle in this year's spring festival, precisely at the stroke of midnight.

The winter frost and bitter cold seemed to seize the final week of December that same year. In the downtown area almost nobody wanted to leave their house after dark and go into the bone-chilling

---

13 The economic reforms initiated in 1986.

air. Only the wind blasted through as leaves tumbled beneath the streetlights. Occasionally, a few people cycled or walked along briskly. Even the evening trolley was almost empty—very few passengers rode in any of the cars.

In the dead of winter, in its tranquility, the rhythms of spring were returning to the city: someone clutching a branch of cherry blossoms, a person ferrying a pot of kumquat behind his bicycle, and buds were already appearing on limbs of barren *bàng* trees. At night, the streets were often empty, but inside the houses lining the main boulevards, one could hear footsteps shuffling and people's voices, or see people busy cooking in their kitchens or cleaning their homes and ancestral altars. December had only twenty-nine days this year, so Tết came sooner, and everybody was in a hurry. Tonight was the 28th, and New Year's Eve was tomorrow.

•

One evening years ago, Năm Tín, an artist from Cà Mau,[14] took the last trolley home after attending a meeting at the Reunification Club with folks from his hometown. He got off the trolley at an intersection. The streetlamp's low light gave it a yellowish color. Every household was so busy making preparations for Tết that no one was sleeping. Light coming from oversized windows illuminated the sidewalks and accompanying street. At the public water pump in front of house No. 3, some women were still busy with washing rice and *dong* leaves. Sounds of water running, buckets clanking. In an empty lot across from the sidewalk at the two-story house No. 4, there was an overflowing cauldron of boiling *bánh chưng*. Hot steam curled around its lid. The fire under the barrel-shaped cauldron was small, but coals spread out over the ground were fiery hot. The children attending the fire moved their mat some distance away because

---

14 The southernmost point of the country.

the heat made them sweat. They played cards, leaving behind a few stragglers to watch the fire. A piece of wood was added to the blaze, making the fire rise higher, brightening their faces and hair, and projecting black shadows against the opposite wall.

Năm Tín was tipsy. With an overstuffed leather bag in his hand, he staggered across the street into the yard of house No. 4. Seeing him, two dogs resting their chins on a sturdy man's thigh quickly jumped up and began barking loudly.

"John and Ken!" the brawny owner of the dogs called out as he stoked the fire. "Knock it off! Don't you recognize Mr. Năm?"

"What's with your vicious mutts today?" Năm Tín said, sitting down and rubbing his chilly, knobby hands by the fire.

The children greeted Năm Tín excitedly. They left their playing cards on the mat and surrounded him.

"This is for me," Năm Tín teased as he opened his leather bag and took out a bottle of Lúa Mới rice wine. "As for you children . . . " He held out a roll of firecrackers wrapped in pink paper that showed a fairy standing on a cloud, and then took out an oversized package emblazoned with Santa Claus wearing a red hat. "We're doing a low-key Tết celebration this year," he went on, "and the Cà Mau People's Association didn't give out a lot of gifts like they usually do every year." He talked as though elucidating some finer point to the kids. "But this is a special treat—candy made in the Soviet Union. The best candy."

"Mr. Năm, you're spoiling the kids," the broad-shouldered man said. "If you give them gifts now, what's left for Tết?" Then, slapping his own thigh, he shouted at the kids, "Behave!"

"It's okay, Trung," Năm Tín said, squeezing the brawny man's shoulder. "No need to get so worked up. But I mean, look at you. Your face looks all messed up. What happened? Did you go a few rounds with somebody in the ring or something?"

"Yes—with hairy Pec," a kid answered.

"They fought because of Giao," another kid added.

"Shut up, you little bastards!" Trung sneered. Only his left eye darted around, as his other eye was bruised and swollen shut above his cut lips. His cheeks were scraped raw.

"Where's Giao?" Năm Tín asked, casting his eyes around.

"I think she's sitting over there crying," another kid, one with close-cropped hair, replied. He pointed toward the balcony on the second floor of the house.

"Why?"

"She's mad at Trung."

"Dear Lord! Bình, you go tell your sister to come down here and talk to me. It's almost the New Year, and we should all be getting along."

Although Năm Tín was an eccentric figure, living in his apartment and not socializing much, he was a good friend of the people living in house No. 4. He often talked only when he had been drinking. But the kids adored him and came by to see him in his house. For example, a few years ago, in the freezing fog of an early morning, they had discovered him lying unconscious and reeking of alcohol in the front yard. They carried him inside, poured a mixture of warm ginger and water into his mouth, and rubbed medicated oil on his body. Afterward, they covered him up with a blanket. When the ambulance came, he had already regained consciousness. Since then, they often visited him in his apartment. They helped him with house chores, carried buckets of water from the public water pump to his apartment, and cleaned up his messy room. Because of this, he pampered them in return. His affection for the children had deepened over the last fifteen years, after military forces from South Việt Nam regrouped in the North. He let them play with his paintings, his pigments, and sketches. He mostly kept to himself and rarely talked about his hometown, but through his paintings, he showed these Hanoian kids his hometown Cà Mau, mothers, women, and children of the revolutionary South, as well as the soldiers of his platoon from 1945 to 1954, which formed part of Battalion 307.

Every year, the five households residing in house No. 4 would prepare for Tết together. The tradition was kept since the day Tá, a truck driver, died. He had a whole litter of children and struggled the most financially of all the families, but he was also the one who made sure everybody living in the house enjoyed Tết. He drove a truck for the Ministry of Forestry and would travel to the Northwest regions. He was never home, except on Tết. Whenever his mud-stained truck pulled up in front of the house and honked noisily, the kids would run out to help him unload firewood, chicken cages, and sacks of both fresh and dehydrated food. Because of him, everybody in the house had enough food to eat during Tết. Unfortunately, Tá had an accident while driving on Pha Đin Pass and died in 1961 during the flood season.

Three families lived downstairs, two upstairs, and everybody struggled to get by. The Tá family and the Thái family, who lived downstairs, had been materially well-off at some point. But then Mr. Thái's life veered off course and he abandoned his wife and children. He took all the money he and his wife had been saving over the years and eloped with another woman and disappeared to Vinh. Their eldest son had to drop out of college. Cư, who also lived downstairs, was once a clerk for the electric company, but he was found guilty of embezzlement and put in jail.

Giao and Bình lived with their grandfather in the room above Mrs. Thái's. Their parents died when the children were very young. This event made their lives miserable. Their sick grandfather was in his seventies, so whether they could enjoy Tết or not depended on his health. Even Professor Xứng's household wasn't ideal. He made a lot of money and his family occupied two big rooms on the second floor. He didn't have many children, but his wife was always sick and she still had to take care of the baby. Their oldest son was in the seventh grade, the youngest just an infant. Their maid had left a month earlier to spend Tết with her family.

Because the adults weren't physically equipped to organize Tết, it was left up to their children. Most of the kids were teenage boys, except for Giao and Trung, the latter being Mrs. Thái's son. So it was up to Giao to handle everything. Her shopping for Tết began at the end of November, and every now and then a few kids gave her a hand after school. She waited in line at state-owned shops from early morning to evening, and it wasn't until the final week prior to Tết that she was able to purchase ingredients like sticky rice and flour, mung beans and bamboo shoots, along with tea, cigarettes, and sweets. But that wasn't the end of it—she had to wait in line again to buy fish sauce, pork, and *dong* leaves to make *bánh chưng*. This year she made sixty *bánh chưng* all by herself. Trung, on the other hand, was in charge of buying the best firewood. He used a sturdy wheelbarrow to transport the wood from Phà Đen to the house and then would spend all afternoon chopping it.

All the preparations took place in the yard. Despite the cold weather, Trung was shirtless and sweaty as he split the firewood with an axe. The other kids were eager to do whatever Trung and Giao asked them, because Tết was a time when they could wear new clothes, eat good food, and play. Next to the public water pump, Giao sat on a bamboo bed covered with plastic and busied herself with wrapping *bánh chưng* in *dong* leaves. She rolled her sleeves up past her elbows. Her ivory hands and arms were flecked with rice grains and mung beans. She didn't wrap *bánh chưng* fast, but her hands moved dexterously, as though she were using a mold. The kids gathered around the bamboo bed to watch her, and then they counted aloud how many she had made. After she had made sixty, she would use the leftover ingredients to make a smaller batch for them.

Earlier that afternoon, when everything was on schedule and almost finished, Vinh from house No. 7 entered the yard and greeted everyone. Vinh's nickname was Pechorin, "a hero of our time,"[15] but

---

15   The Byronic hero in the 1839 novel *A Hero of Our Time*, written by Russian author Mikhail Lermontov.

he was known mostly as Pec, because even though he was young, he had hairy forearms and a full beard.

Only Giao glanced up and acknowledged Pec. Trung said nothing. He clenched his teeth as wood splinters flew all around him. The kids took Trung's side, so they turned their attention to him. The dogs, John and Ken, jumped down from the porch, barked, and rushed toward Pec, even though Giao ordered them not to. Pec stomped his foot on the ground and the dogs scurried away. The kids also scattered. Pec strolled up to Giao. He was wearing a Czech leather jacket, a pair of corduroy pants, and patent leather shoes. He was an imposing figure, athletic, with neatly cropped hair combed back. His nose was rigid, his lips were full, and he sported a beard. His parents owned a jewelry shop, which meant they didn't have to worry about money much, though Pec didn't mooch off them. He was currently an apprentice in Mr. Tạ Duy Hiển's circus.[16] Pec was considered the most eligible bachelor in town.

"Giao, you're so good at making *bánh chưng*. They are perfectly square," Pec complimented. He picked up a pair of her *bánh chưng* and added, "Maybe you can come to my house next year and make some for us."

Pec was a sociable person, neighborly, so he was well liked by everyone in the neighborhood—with the exception of the boys living in the house. On the afternoon he visited Giao, he had no intention of provoking Trung. In fact, Pec was allowed to spend time with her. Everybody knew that Pec's parents had consulted with Giao's grandfather. Although Pec and Giao were not yet engaged, both families had allowed their children to get to know each other. She didn't know what her grandfather thought about him, but she found him charming and affable herself.

Pec took out two colorful invitations folded inside his pocket and showed them to Giao. It was the 28th of December, and the Tân

---

16 Tạ Duy Hiển (1889–1967), the founding father of the modern Vietnamese circus.

Cương artists were having their opening night performance later. The event was free, but theatergoers needed a formal invitation.

"We've got front row seats for seven o'clock," he said. "Please get your work done soon so you have time to get ready. You may need to dress up, since it'll be at the Opera House. I'll pick you up around six."

Trung, holding an axe, started to feel provoked. He walked toward Giao while ignoring Pec and growled, "Theater? You've still got all this rice here that you haven't even finished washing yet. When can we cook *bánh chưng*?"

"It's all done. I made sixty *bánh chưng*," she said. "All you need to do is put them in the pot. Why are you so worried? It's still early."

"Early, huh? There's tons of work left. If you keep talking to this guy, it'll be midnight before we're done. You'll end up chatting with him until morning."

"She's been slaving away and needs time off, too," Pec interrupted. "It's Tết. Don't be so bossy!"

Trung said nothing. Then, suddenly, he hurled the axe and lodged it in the ground right next to Pec's feet. Startled, Pec sprang back and nearly fell over. Giao was appalled and left speechless. Nobody else said a word.

"Get out of here, you spoiled bastard!" Trung said. "If you keep bothering her, you'll be spending Tết in the hospital!"

Pec became livid. His voice crackled with anger. "You're acting hysterical. I haven't done anything to you. Why are you yelling at me?"

"I'll teach you a lesson," Trung said, suddenly taking a swing at Pec.

Pec dodged the punch by stepping to one side. He thumped Trung on the chest. "Knock it off, Trung," he warned. "You don't want this."

Pec played all kinds of sports, but he was especially good at boxing. He laughed at Trung's attempt to hit him. Even if Trung was strong, he wasn't an experienced fighter. Pec then threw a punch at Trung, hitting him in the mouth, knocking him over. Trung, who was shirtless, was now covered in filth as he struggled to get back on his feet. He was drenched in sweat and bleeding. Pec didn't follow through with another blow. Instead, he unzipped his leather jacket, tossed it aside, and rolled up his shirtsleeves. Trung, gathering all his courage and strength, clenched his teeth and, with a head as hard as a coconut, head-butted Pec right in the stomach. Pec fell over onto the bamboo bench. Trung lunged forward and pinned his knees on Pec's chest. Biting his bottom lip, he started bashing Pec in the face. Nobody uttered a word during the bloody fight.

One of the kids helped lift Giao to her feet. Color drained from her face as she begged for the fighting to stop, but nobody seemed to pay her any attention. The fight only intensified.

"Please stop! Oh, God, stop fighting!" she yelled, jerking her hand away from the kid who had helped her up. Finally, she broke up the fight by yanking on Trung's hair, forcing him to take his hands off Pec.

The fight lasted only a few minutes. Trung, taking shallow breaths, stood up. His face was streaked with blood. One of his eyes was swollen shut. The other eye was completely red. He clenched his fists and gnashed his teeth, wanting to murder Giao.

"You're so terrible," she said, choking back her words. She burst into tears and ran back into the house.

•

But Trung didn't take out his anger on Giao. He put more *bánh chưng* into the pot and stoked the fire. The kids went back to playing cards to pass the time. Everyone seemed settled except for Giao; she refused to come down to hang out with the others. Without her, there would be no laughter or festive stories, no apples or baked corn. Without her presence, Trung lost his interest in most everything and sat there unmoving like a rock. Since the fight, he talked only briefly with a local policeman working the night shift and a street sweeper who stopped by the fire to warm up. By the time Năm Tín came around, the youngest kids had dozed off and only the older ones sat attending the fire with Trung.

Bình, Giao's younger brother, ran upstairs and tried to convince her to come back down, but she was determined not to go downstairs and confront Trung again. She told Bình to take some drinking glasses and a plate of roasted squid to Năm Tín. After that, he would need to come back to carry down blankets, a basket of apples, and ten ears of corn to the other kids.

"Trung, you can drink with me," Năm Tín said, pouring wine into two glasses. "You're a man now."

Trung shook his head. The old man shrugged and downed the glass quickly. "Men are like tigers, you know," he said. "We don't hold grudges. You'll soon be leaving for military service, so make peace with Pec."

Then he filled his glass with more wine and emptied it again. He gave the plate of what was left of the roasted squid to the kids and polished off both bottles of Lúa Mới wine.

Trung said nothing. After their bellies were full, the kids fell asleep on the mat, one after another. Eventually, the dogs lay down beside them. The water in the pot boiled unattended as the fire hissed and crackled. Before long, the streets and houses fell into darkness. The sky clouded over and the temperature dropped. Although the wind had stopped blowing some time ago, a frigid cold filled the air. Dawn was coming soon.

"I have to go," Năm Tín finally said after many hours of silence. He picked up his empty leather bag and staggered to his feet. Trung tried to assist him.

"No need," he declined. "I'm not drunk. Really, I'm not." The old man, smelling strongly of booze, embraced Trung. "You're leaving on the fifth, aren't you? Well, I hope you have a safe time. I've got to go now, Trung. I need to get home and set up a shrine for my parents, my wife, and my children for Tết." Then he started to choke up and his eyes were wet. His whole body quaked as though struggling for air.

"Trung, they killed all of my family. They killed everybody . . . my youngest daughter Út, my sons Hai and Ba. All three were killed at the same time. Then they killed my mother, my father. They killed my wife. What savage animals! Two years ago now. I attended a meeting yesterday afternoon, you know, and a man from my hometown who just got here told me the news."

He sobbed as he told Trung about the tragedy. Then he pulled himself away from Trung and, using the wall, slumped toward the other end of town.

Early the next morning, Giao came downstairs and brought extra blankets for the kids. She told Trung to go to his room and get some sleep. She would tend the fire for him. He sat there and said nothing. Although she was upset and was about to walk back inside, she sat down by the fire instead, away from him.

A kid who had his blanket taken away woke up. He heard Trung say something about Năm Tín. Then he heard Giao crying. The kid craned his neck to eavesdrop in the darkness. The whole scene fell into silence again. He watched the young couple sitting next to the fire, holding each other and crying. Her flowing hair was untied, her sweater unbuttoned. He saw Trung kiss her neck and embrace her. He could feel the heat coming from the fire as he exhaled into the cold, early morning air. The kid couldn't understand why she always hung out with Pec, especially that following day, on New Year's Eve, and later during Tết when he took Giao on his burgundy Piaggio bicycle to music performances and fairs. Pec's face was left bruised after the fight, but he lost none of his charming looks.

●

In the early afternoon on the fifth day after Tết, a farewell ceremony for newly enlisted soldiers took place at the bottom of Đống Đa Hillock. It was said that for the past ten years, ever since peace was largely restored, Hà Nội had never experienced such a huge number of volunteers like this. Hundreds were ready to join the war, and thousands of people came to say goodbye. As the sea of people rose and sang the national anthem, a Tây Sơn flag[17] and another flag with a gold star were slowly raised up together in front of the Trung Liệt Memorial. A first lieutenant read aloud the names of the enlisted men. Each volunteer present said "Here" when his name was called. The officer read names until he lost his voice, and even after that the list still had not been exhausted. Whenever Trung heard a familiar name, he perked up and surveyed the crowd. But this was a massive group, so there was no way he could find people he recognized.

Trung looked around. It seemed like all the girls in town were here, and they looked more beautiful than he had remembered. They were hugging each other and talking cheerfully as they stood in small clusters next to the men. After the recruitment ceremony, he thought, the town would probably be left with only young women and children. Trung's mother and three younger siblings, as well as all the kids living in house No. 4, also came to say goodbye to him. It was already late in the afternoon, but the event seemed to have no end in sight. Later on, Trung told his siblings to take their mother home, but she refused to leave. She had an anemic look about her, fumbling as she tried to latch tightly onto Trung's hand. Choking back tears, she told him repeatedly to take care of himself, but couldn't find the right words to express her raw feelings.

"Mom, quit acting like this," he said, feeling embarrassed. "Everybody's staring at us . . ." Then he turned to the children and said, "You guys take care of her for me, okay? Try to keep her from crying at home later. Help her with the chores. I'll be gone for three

---

17 A national movement in the late eighteenth century, often known as the Tây Sơn rebellion, led by three brothers Nguyễn Huệ, Nguyễn Nhạc, Nguyễn Lữ. "The revolt initially had a broad social base, drawing from peasant and merchant classes, and sought political and social reforms. The brothers have been regarded by many historians as precursors of the twentieth-century Vietnamese nationalist movement." (www.britannica.com)

years, but I'm allowed to take leave. Make sure you guys take care of our house and that apple tree I planted. By the time I come back, the tree, hopefully, should be as tall as the balcony."

Although Trung put on a cheerful face while talking, he seemed heartbroken as he looked around. The kids loved him but that didn't make him feel any better. Only Giao did, but her grandfather had been hospitalized the night before, so she was there looking after him. On top of that, Pec was always by her side.

The cold spring air revealed a blue sky. After the speeches, musical performances, and poetry recitals, the new recruits boarded buses. Nearly twenty buses snaked along one side of the square. Their engines started up and noisy honking followed. Trung embraced his mother and his siblings, along with each of the children living in the building, for the last time.

"Please don't cry," Trung said to them. "Don't cry, so I can leave. Just take my mom home." Then he said to her, "Mom, I have to leave now. Please go home."

Trung threw his rucksack through the bus window and climbed aboard the bus. A huge crowd swelled around the bus, but somehow Mrs. Thái, his mother, was able to push her way through and stood directly beneath his window.

"Mom!" Trung reached out for her hands awkwardly, but their fingers slipped apart as other people closed in.

"Is that you, Toàn? Hey, Toàn!" his mother sobbed. He was Trung's friend and lived in house No. 36, on the same block. "Toàn, please look after him for me," his mother said.

The bus lurched forward. People in the crowd called out to their loved ones, cheered them on, and even wept. Suddenly, out in the middle of the mob, Trung saw Giao.

Trung somehow, miraculously, forced his way off the bus.

"Giao!" he said. "Over here, I'm over here!"

"Where are you?" she shouted as she pushed her way through the mass of bodies. "Where are you?"

Giao slipped several times, unable to see him, or anything else. She started to feel dizzy. But, finally spotting Trung, she caught her breath and ran toward him. He pushed people aside and threw his arms tightly around her.

Unlike at previous farewell ceremonies, most of the volunteers this time were around Trung's age. They were still very young, so it was rare to see wives saying goodbye to husbands; but there were several young lovers like Trung and Giao. Although what they felt could be called love—inhibited and modest as they were—it was an innocent kind of love. Not until this very moment of separation did they dare express their affections.

Giao's hair spilled down her back. She leaned her body into Trung and wrapped her arms around his neck, embracing him in front of everyone. He held her tightly, his large hands reaching beneath her sweater. People heaved a sympathetic sigh, but averted their eyes. All the buses started to move again. Singing could be heard from the bus in front, booming throughout town:

Those who cross Cửu Long Giang River see its swift waters,
Those who hear of war know Battalion 307,
On the day we men celebrate our leaving,
We give allegiance to the red flag with a yellow star . . .

In the street, Trung was running after the last bus. Several hands extended out the back door to help pull him aboard. Giao ran behind frantically, as fast as she could. She lost her footing and fell on the slippery ground.

Hà Nội girls may be poor,
But are the most enchanting fairies,
With ivory skin, crimson lips,
Charcoal eyes, and willowy eyelashes . . .

Once, I heard a song with these lines somewhere, but can't remember when. I was just a little boy living in house No. 4 on that Memorial Day afternoon when I said goodbye to Trung at the bottom of Đống Đa Hillock; I was the same boy who helped Giao to her feet. She was sobbing and trembling violently in my arms. On our way back home, I calmly consoled her. She held her face as she walked, not caring that people were staring. From what I remember since that day, nobody ever looked as fragile or wretched as she did then.

•

Months and years afterward, I attended many events like that, but I never forgot that time when my friends and I said goodbye to Trung. Five years later, I also enlisted and joined the war. It was mostly peaceful by the beginning of 1964, but young men were still expected to perform military service. Among the middle class, even our wise elders couldn't tell what the future held, whereas I was just a thirteen-year-old boy. As I now gaze back toward that time, I don't remember imagining how anything could be different.

The truth of it was, during that particularly tranquil spring day when Trung left, my heart was troubled as I stood at the bottom of Đống Đa Hillock. I wasn't the only one who felt this way, and I sensed it in the people around me too, my friends and other strangers, who had until now sought a peaceful existence. But we could feel the waves of a new age crashing on the shores of our Fatherland—a modern era characterized by extraordinary events and sorrow of historic proportions. It was to be our age of struggle, our age of revolution, our age of endless heartbreak and unspeakable loss; but it was also to be our age of everlasting heroism, of survival—our age of love and resolute courage.

The artist Năm Tín, Trung, his mother, Giao, and the kind and fragile-hearted women living in house No. 4, as well as my feelings about the fate of my countrymen, inspired in me a deep, lasting change, even before I had entered adulthood. For me, my happy

and beautiful childhood ended on that gorgeous spring afternoon of 1964.

A week after Tết, my father received a raise and we were offered a
better place to live. We moved to the downtown area of the city. In
August of that year, the Americans bombed the North. Everybody
in my school evacuated to the countryside. We didn't have a chance
to visit Hà Nội often, and even when we did, we didn't stay long.
Then I joined the military and headed South without knowing the
day of my return. Such was my destiny back then.

•

Returning to Hà Nội after the war ended, I saw only reminders of that
previous struggle all around me; the wind had, in that time, blown
the prewar years away. Now and then I passed by the old part of town
and my old house, and at first I didn't care to look at it, feeling only a
detachment and aloofness. Later, I felt deep ambivalence whenever I
passed by the old house. The house had not changed over the years,
but appeared only slightly more battered, with its facade full of cracks
and paint peeling off its walls. It was squalid-looking, full of rattling
sounds, and overcrowded, as there were far too many new tenants
living there. But I was glad to see Trung's apple tree, the one he had
planted before enlisting. It had grown taller than the balcony and cast
a long shadow over the yard. The tree itself looked very old, even if
nobody would eat the kind of apples it produced these days.

This year, during Tết, as I walked from my new house to house
No. 4, I noticed that the apple tree was gone. Tấn, Trung's youngest
brother and a veteran of the border wars, had been allowed by the
municipal authorities to enlarge his property into the yard. Although
he had no desire to chop down the tree, he felt an obligation to do it.

"During the war," Tấn told me sadly, "we dug public trenches in
the yard, so we were able to keep the tree. But now I've got to let it go.
It makes me sad, but what can I do?"

When I asked about Giao, he replied, "She and her husband left for Sài Gòn to spend Tết there. They'll most likely move to the South for good very soon."

•

A month after Tết, in February, I went to visit Giao, and by a stroke of good fortune she was home. Previously, she was always on business trips when I tried to see her. The last time we met face-to-face was thirty-four years ago. She was still living in the same room with the balcony facing the street. The walls were coated in lime plaster and blue curtains hung in the windows. The ancestral altar inside had three perpetually burning incense sticks. When she opened the door to let me in, the light had not yet been turned on, so the red sunset engulfed the room. Giao was the same person I had known in my youth. She recognized me and called me by my nickname. It broke my heart to see her.

Giao sat down next to me and wept for a long time. I was also crying, and my eyes felt as though pricked by pins. Outside, the cityscape was all lit up. We held each other's hand and sat in that dark room, letting a serene feeling overcome us, as we cherished the memories of our youth. Our voices trembled as we recounted to each other our lives since then. Her life and my life were not so different from those of our countrymen for the past several years, but when we spoke about the distant past, our hearts filled with sorrow. In any case, we were able to temper our mood and keep our composure.

"Do you remember Mr. Năm, the artist?" she asked.

"Of course. But I haven't seen him in decades. How's he doing?"

"He died back in 1990, in his hometown in the South. He headed south in 1971, and I never saw him again. He visited Hà Nội not long before he passed away, but I wasn't home. He met Vinh, my husband, and left me a gift . . ."

"Vinh?" I shuddered. "How come your husband is *also* named Vinh?"

Back in our younger days, the tough-looking Pec, whose real name was Vinh, was infatuated with Giao. He later died in the cruel, dry season of 1972. He lost his life in front of my eyes. My squad had followed his T54 tank and attacked the Plầy Cần military base. Just as we entered the base and were about to pull out our bayonets and jump off the tank, two Mecar M72 LAW anti-tank rockets hit us and killed almost everybody. The tank caught on fire.

"I've asked other artists about him, but nobody remembers him," Giao said of Năm Tín, "as he wasn't in their league." She reached up and turned on the overhead light. The single lightbulb glowed softly, like a candle. She said in a low voice, "Come here," and stood up from her chair and gently took my hand. She led me to the curtained window, where an oil painting hung on the wall in a brown, wooden frame.

My knees went weak as I approached the painting. I felt something rise from the pit of my heart. Looking at it, I was at a loss for words. The painting depicted seven of us, the children of house No. 4, sitting by the fire on the night of the 28th prior to the Tết of the Year of the Dragon. There was a powerful mood to the scene. The red aura of the dancing flames brightened our faces. Radiating outward, the flames seemed to struggle against the night. The sky that night, I remember, was not dark but rather clear. Above us were the heavens in all their magnificence and solemnity, a dark sky belonging to an extraordinary time that nobody could reclaim. In the painting, I saw the familiar scene of my youth, of a house diminished over time.

Those familiar faces buoyed by the fire gave the painting a soul. The artist's hypnotic strokes filled me with sorrow—a sorrow that transported me back to the past and burrowed itself deep into my heart. A new truth also dawned on me, something I was not aware of until this moment because of my callousness and poor judgment. Of the seven portrayed in the painting, back when we were just foolish children sitting around a fire, I was *the only one* to live; everyone else was now dead.

•

Last year, on Ancestors' Day in March, I passed through Gio Linh and stopped to visit the Trường Sơn Fallen Soldiers' Cemetery. I found the name of Giao's brother, Bình, among thousands of headstones, in an area where they buried soldiers from Hà Nội. Giao and her husband had wanted to bring Bình's remains back to the capital, but one night she had a dream in which her brother told her he wanted to lie along with his comrades in the red-soiled *le* forest where they had fought. In the painting, he is just ten years old and looks somewhat like Giao with his smooth skin and bewitching face. He is hollow-cheeked, his hair curly, and his lips sulky as he sits with his arms wrapped around his knees.

Sitting next to Bình is Phái, who was twelve, with a buzz cut that reveals a misshapen head hatched with scars. His high cheekbones expose a wide mouth, his pallid face full of pockmarks. In the painting, he frowns with furrowed eyebrows. He was the eldest son of Tá, the truck driver. Although Phái wore shabby clothes and was the least attractive among us boys, he remained kind and forgiving. Both of us had joined the military in 1969. I was an infantryman, and he became an anti-aircraft gunner. He was stationed in Hà Nội and died there, in the twelve-day battle against B-52 bombers.

Sơn, Cư's son, was the only one in his family to go to college, although his father was in prison. In the painting, he is just a short kid, only a year older than me, and sits cross-legged. He has disheveled hair and is scrawny as a runt. There is an unpolished look about him, but his round, moonlike eyes reveal the intelligence beneath. He sits next to the cauldron of boiling *bánh chưng* and looks lost in his own thoughts, as though trying to do sums in his head. Sơn passed his college entrance exams and became a math major, but he dropped out of college his sophomore year and enlisted instead. He became an artilleryman and died at Chum Field.

In a shadowy corner of the painting is Đính, Trung's younger brother. A blanket is wrapped around his body and he sits a good distance from the fire. With his hands propping up his chin, he doesn't resemble his brother at all. Đính's cheeks have retained their baby fat. His ears are too large, his jowls pointy, and his neck too narrow for his head. His demeanor, as well, makes him different from his brother. Unlike his brother, Đính had been an unassertive boy, but eleven years later, in the dry season of 1975, he was among the soldiers in the commando company that attacked the Hòa Bình Airport on the outskirts of Buôn Mê Thuột, which paved the way for the Great Revolution. He perished along with most of his comrades before our infantrymen and tanks could arrive to help.

Trung, Đính's brother, is drawn most clearly in the painting. He sits cross-legged in the erect posture of a monk, his chest puffing out a little. Two yellow dogs flank him and rest their heads on his thighs. I have rarely met a man since then who was as strong and resilient as Trung. He looks short in the painting, but also is portrayed as barrel-chested and with abs like a washboard. His broad shoulders and chiseled physique bulge from under his blue Maritime shirt. He has a high forehead and a flattened nose; his cheekbones jut out, revealing an angular chin; his stumpy neck makes his oversized head appear even larger beneath his close-cropped hair. The firelight turns his skin bronze. Giao used to tease him, calling him Kettle Boy.

The artist did not portray Trung's swollen face and belligerent character. Indeed, he comes across as a young man full of conviction and untapped potential. But in the painting, he looks deeply contemplative. In his wide-open eyes there is a preoccupation with some kind of otherworldliness, a deep sadness, as though wanting to speak something unspeakable. Trung was the first anti-American soldier from house No. 4 to lose his life, most likely the first in his neighborhood if not the whole city. He joined the marines and died at sea on a stormy day in early August 1964, in Hòn Mê. The news of his death came to town long before his official death notification. In

1970, when Pec joined the military, Giao was still waiting patiently for Trung's return. Pec had told me about it on the night our units were stationed in an old forest by Highway 18, awaiting our orders to attack Plây Cần.

"I know Giao is torn by love," he had said, only half-jokingly. "She loves both Trung and me paradoxically, but Trung enlisted first, so she thinks she loves him more. But if my death notification letter arrives before Trung's, she will realize where her love actually lies."

In the painting, Giao sits in the light of the dancing fire, an image as spirited as it is mysterious. The artist included her in the painting, though she didn't join the kids in attending the fire that night. The artist chose not to paint her sitting beside Trung but next to another boy instead, their bodies folded together, the pair sitting distant from the other subjects in the painting.

Giao, in the painting, is seventeen. Haloed by the light's soft glow, her rosy, oval face blooms with beauty. She bites her bottom lip slightly; her swan-like neck pale as ivory. She sits with her head bowed, her arms around her knees. With her head down it's impossible to see her eyes, but her eyebrows unveil dewy lashes. Giao looks inconsolable in the painting. The boy sitting next to her is tall with spidery legs, and he wears leather shoes and a fur-lined coat. He obviously comes from a better family, economically, than the other kids in the painting. His face is inconspicuous, his body leaning against hers, and his arms embracing her by the waist. He has his head resting on her shoulder with his face buried in her long, angelic hair. I remember looking at him earnestly and feeling a chill. Was it me? Carefully, that evening at Giao's residence, I approached the canvas, trying to control my emotions. But as I examined the painting more closely, all the details of the scene became broad strokes, and all I could see were splotches of color and the hand of the artist.

I stepped back, and standing at a good distance from the artwork, the painterly slashes and pigments and patches of color coalesced, revealing to me all my fellow comrades who had died, as well as me and Giao. I was the one who had buried my head in her hair that night. I had never sat like that before and never acted that way since, but I know I had dreamed about it many times. What kind of mysterious power causes such hidden memories to materialize in this painting before my eyes?

•

I enjoyed no romantic love throughout my younger years. As a teenager until the day I enlisted, then during my six years in the battlefield, I was never intimate with a woman. Campaign after campaign, in dry season after wet, all my energy was invested in marches, fighting in the trenches, and utter devotion to my comrades. But sometimes, in the early morning, when there was no bombing or artillery fire, I would wake up in the forest and find myself swinging in my hammock, drowned in a memory that wasn't mine. In this other phantasmagorical world of my own invention, I had seen myself, and not Trung, embracing Giao firmly in the midst of that massive crowd at the bottom of Đống Đa Hillock, or by the fire in the yard of our house. In some corner of that forest, speechless, I had dreamed about her brushing up against my chest as my hands reached out for her rounded breasts, and imagined kissing her lips and smelling the perfume of her body and the scent of her hair. But I knew that they were only forbidden fantasies that would eventually crush my soul. I didn't want to suffer any further heartache, but are we not mortal, and if so, how do we control our desires?

After the war ended, when those sinful fantasies were gone, I realized that my sin had to do with my first love; even if that love had never existed in the real world, it was a sin nevertheless. I was foolish and naive, but in that imaginary first love, which I had buried deep in my heart, I was encouraged by its uplifting promise. It was why, I believe, I had survived the war and returned from it safely. Even more so, that illusory first love became a source of hope that helped me in conducting my life after I returned from the war, to live courageously, happily, and overcome those long years of struggle in the postwar period.

Back in the room with the painting on that night, Giao had sighed and said, "Next week, I'm going back to Sài Gòn, probably for good. My husband has moved there and likes it. I was unsure, but he's very adamant that I *either* move there and join him and our children, *or*..."

We stood on the spacious balcony surrounded by a few potted flowers. The spring air was chilly and a light rain fell.

"Please take part of the apple tree home with you when you have time," Giao said, pointing to what was left of the tree in a shady corner of the yard. "Before Tấn chopped down the tree, he took off a cutting for me. I didn't expect it to live, but it's growing now. See its roots? If you want, you can take the cutting home with you and put it in a pot. Take care of it. Then, after a while, you can plant it in the ground so that it grows to full maturity. For me, I love Vietnamese apples. People used to prefer imported Western apples, but for Tết this year, they want Vietnamese apples."

Giao talked in a wistful, soothing voice. It was getting very cold outside on the balcony, but neither of us wanted to go back inside. As night encroached, the temperature dropped even more, but I felt no chill at all. Instead, a kind of warmth radiated from deep inside my body. Standing right next to Giao, I thought I could stand there forever.

"I will leave this room to Tấn," she said. "His family had three brothers. All of them went to war, but Tấn was the only one to return alive. I'll leave him the painting, too. His family doesn't have any photos of Trung, and this painting is the only one I know with him in it." Seeing me light a cigarette, Giao asked, "Are you a smoker now?"

I laughed. Thirty-five years ago, she had coyly reprimanded me for smoking when she caught me hiding under the stairwell with one of my father's cigarettes.

In that dark room, she looked more youthful than ever, and I felt it, too. As the day ended and with another about to begin, at exactly the stroke of midnight, we were transported back to the Hà Nội of our youth and to our friends—the ones who were now already dead. We were brought back to our innocent childhood, our first inkling of love. Our generation was born, came of age, worked, and fought in the war. We had sacrificed for our city, and we were beneficiaries of its miracles. We have become, since then, a generation forever trapped by our innocence, in a young and unchanging city.

Untamed Winds

"Listen! It is Diệu Nương's voice."

Although several months, or years, have now passed since Diệu Nương was shot to death, the people of Diêm Village still hear her voice. Each dawn, half-asleep, they tell each other to go looking for her, as though the past speaks to them again.

I wander through life without a past,
Ashore, I dream, awaiting your footsteps.

Dawn comes quietly, and the Morning Star, more luminous and loftier than ever above the grasslands, burns through the unblemished heavens. Before the sun rises, along the fertile prairie, fog and darkness uncoil and fade away. It is in this faint light that a village gradually reveals itself.

A long scar on Road 14.[18] A clump of tin-roof shanties. A church.

The incessant crowing of roosters and the water wells' creaky pulleys awaken Diêm Village. The village, opening its eyes, rises alone, marooned on this boundless and forsaken land. On the other side of

---

18 The most important and longest road in the former South Việt Nam that ran parallel to the Trường Sơn Mountains and the Việt Nam–Laos border.

the plain, inside the South Vietnamese Army Corps II military base, the 105 mm M102 howitzers lie silent. Nowhere on the horizon can the Cessna L-19 Bird Dog[19] be spotted. One lonely supply truck hurries across the A Rang River that runs through the village, splashing circles that gradually die away on the calm water. It is the dry season.

Throughout the night, Road 14 was swarmed with military trucks and troops marching by the church through the village. By dawn, they were all gone. Now the streets are empty. On a dirt road veiled by fog, oxcarts carry farmers to the field—the sound of wood clopping as their wheels turn over the ground. Here and there a scatter of fog-enshrouded houses with tin roofs, the smoke from their hearths vanishing into the air. Somewhere beyond the layers of fog, as the dim sky kisses the riverbank and the grassy plain farewell, a soulful voice lifts up through the air with help from a dying wind.

I wander through life without a past.

Some time ago, while the church bell rang its Catholic parishioners to morning Mass, the bell tower was hit by an artillery shell. No sound has been heard from it since. Bomb craters now pockmark the churchyard, but no one cares to fill them. Thorny, overgrown bushes sprout wildly along the footpaths. Every morning, on the stone steps leading to the front door of the church, a Catholic priest in his black cassock quietly leans against the entrance and gazes toward the rising sun.

The priest's heart is heavy with sorrow, as though charged by an almighty power. He quickly makes the sign of the cross, shrugs, then bows his head with closed eyes. He sighs to himself.

In the distance, a soft, yolk-like golden sun leisurely climbs the low eastern hills of the plain. The sunlight, cascading down the horizon, turns the sky a magnificent blue. At the start of this new day, Diệu

---

19 Observation aircraft.

Nương's voice seems to grow and resonate everywhere like a hymn, indistinct from the melody of creation.

The adults of the village are appalled when children sing along with Diệu Nương.

Meanwhile, on the far side of the river in an anti-aircraft battery that protects the underwater passage for vehicles, artillerymen prepare for a daylong battle. Suddenly they stop working. They give up surveilling the sky and train their binoculars on the village.

Oh, unholy moon . . .

"Look, it's her!" a soldier cries out, pointing his finger at an apparition.

Everything looks unfocused through the lens of the binoculars. There appears to be a woman singing beyond the undergrowth covering the narrow road that circles the village. Her hair spills down her slender body as she gracefully moves, a mirage created in song, a ghost, however enchanting and animated, who can vanish inexplicably without a trace. The real and the fantastical blur into one another, sounds and images indistinguishable. The legend of Diệu Nương, a Saigonese singer who was trapped in the liberated zone, is a daily topic of interest to the men of this artillery battalion, with each man embellishing the legend in his own way. Standing on the roof of the communications bunker, the commander of the company and the political instructor pass the binoculars back and forth.

"*Wander through life!*" the political instructor says, repeating the words from the song. He frowns, pulling down his binoculars. "We'd better shut that whore up or the entire company will be seduced by her voice. She'll trick our men and lead them astray."

"But how can we get her to stop?" the commander asks, shrugging his shoulders.

"We'll find a way," the political instructor says. "No saccharine songs, no anti-revolutionary songs, no *ngụy*[20] songs."

"But Trịnh Công Sơn[21] wrote that song."

"That makes no difference. I don't know why she always sings around this time. Is it a signal to someone? A way to lure our men into her bed, so they lose their will to fight? Is that what she's doing?"

"But her voice is divine."

Past the river, a group of infantrymen walk through fields of feathery cogon grass, their weapons glinting light. The man at the very back stops, turns his head around, and looks back toward Diêm Village.

Vapor rises from the ashen waters of the A Rang River. A song carried by the wind fills the soldier's heart and sends a chill down his spine. Her voice is clear, as though bathed in the unspoiled morning, but in its echo a sound more sorrowful, an expression of the land's primordial spirit. The voice is unbridled, just like the boundless land, free, its hymn spreading to unreachable vistas, over fields that know nothing of war and struggle, death and slaughter.

•

How sad that rootless singing! How sea-deep that sorrow!

Despite how often people embellish or glorify the legend, Diệu Nương's life still remains a mystery. Many were certain that she came to the A Rang River in the summer of 1972, after the Liberation Army launched their attack on Saigonese troops and forced them to retreat. Before that, very few people knew who she was, where she came from, or even her name, and those who claimed to know about her told unfounded stories. Even Diệu Nương, having forgotten everything about herself, didn't know who she was.

---

20 A derogatory term the Vietnamese communists used to refer to the "puppet" South Vietnamese government, its supporters, or its arts and literature.
21 Trịnh Công Sơn (1939–2001) is well known for his love songs and antiwar songs.

She had no clothes on when she first came here. I heard the same thing, and that during the Easter Offensive of 1972—during the Red Fiery Summer[22]—she wasn't the only one to witness horror. Humans are like trees and grass. War, like fields set ablaze, can burn us to ash in a single moment.

Many people were killed back in 1972. Corpses were found lying everywhere in the streets, in the grassy fields, and even floating on the river. Those who survived the catastrophe looked more dead than alive. The land was left in ruins, the village a shadow of itself.

Before that tragedy, the village was bustling and prosperous; houses crowded each other. The village lay about ten kilometers from the town,[23] as the crow flies, when the Americans defended it. Men from the village enlisted and were paid for their military service; women sold things at the market. The entire village was religious and went to church. But then the thriving village, under the Americans, was reduced to rubble.

Distant cannons pounded the village every day, and planes dropped bombs on its river and fields. The iron bridge crossing the A Rang River was destroyed. The bombardment intensified after sappers began transporting rocks to build the underwater passageway. Life was disrupted.

By the middle of 1973, the NVA anti-aircraft Battalion 17 arrived to defend the underwater passageway of the A Rang River. Three

---

22 "Many Americans probably believed that by 1972, the war in Vietnam was essentially winding down. However, for the US Navy in Vietnam, 1972 would prove to be a busy year of conducting numerous and dangerous combat operations. An example of events that year happened in late March 1972, with an action taken by North Vietnam that came to be officially called 'The 1972 Spring–Summer Offensive.' Certain South Vietnamese literature refers to it as 'Red Fiery Summer,' since this campaign by North Vietnam was sustained through the spring/summer months until October of 1972" (George Trowbridge, https://georgetrowbridges8b.com/2018/11/15/easter-offensive-of-1972/).

23 This refers to Kon Tum, a town (now a city) in the Central Highlands, south-central Việt Nam.

anti-aircraft companies were stationed on both sides of the river to fight against the South Vietnamese Air Force. At the time, my company was stationed alongside Diêm Village, ghostly back then, and everywhere covered with weeds, thorny bushes, and piles of shattered bricks and broken poles. Here and there in the rubble were collapsed huts and shanty houses. Dogs scavenged in mountains of garbage, where the refuse of some previous existence lay exposed: torn, colorful clothing, tattered dresses, leather scraps and plastic, shards of broken glass, household possessions, and even human and animal bones the dogs had dug up and ravaged.

After that, the population of the village dwindled and its wounded inhabitants were displaced. Not many men survived and those who did were ignored or forgotten—disabled veterans who became blind and miserable cripples. Only children and women were seen outside the home. The children were emaciated and left without clothes. The war widows, whose backgrounds and origins remained a mystery, were skeletons in rags. The people now living in Diêm Village, for the most part, were not the original inhabitants. In the summer of 1972, they had migrated from surrounding towns, villages, and military districts by following Road 14, reaching as far as Diêm Village before tanks of the Liberation Army stopped them. And it was here, one midnight, that many were massacred.

As the story goes, when they heard the roar of a Dakota transport plane overhead, the terrified refugees took up thousands of torches and howled at the Noah's Ark hovering overhead. In the churchyard, the villagers made an enormous fiery cross. Nobody heard the sound of the aircraft as it disappeared, dropping flares that lit the horizon like lightning. The airstrike lasted until early the next morning and countless people, their cries drowned out by the sounds of war, died. By a stroke of luck, Diệu Nương was among those who survived.

Afterward, the survivors became Diêm Village's new inhabitants, with little choice but to start new lives there. They didn't complain about their new reality, their struggle toiling the fields, or their hunger and misery. Everybody had to follow the rules established by the new Communist government. Those who stubbornly resisted were brought to heel. Some were even shot to death, many more imprisoned.

Diệu Nương was later arrested and jailed by guerrillas. They confined her in an underground cell because she sang *ngụy* songs. After her release, she isolated herself from society but continued to live on her own terms. She sang as a matter of habit, her voice like a siren's song. Every night, it is rumored, men came to her dilapidated hut by the shores of the river. They either knocked on her wooden door or raked their hands along her bamboo walls. They brought dehydrated rations with them, satchels of rice, canned meat, cigarettes, sewing kits, mirrors and combs, even saltpeter in the hope that she might take them to her bed. Although there was no proof, Diệu Nương earned the ignominy of being branded a scandalous woman, and because of this, rumors began to spread that she had once been a bar girl on an American military base. Even worse, some called her a prostitute. But it was only hearsay; nobody really knew who she was.

It is said that she had been a famous Sài Gòn singer once. One night in 1972, her band had agreed to perform for the South Vietnamese Rangers Corps, but their final number coincided with the onset of the Communist Red Fiery Summer campaign. North Vietnamese tanks and infantry invaded Tân Trấn. The South Vietnamese defense line was broken, soldiers were slaughtered, and as a result, Diệu Nương's bandmates scattered everywhere. She followed the stampede of people out and quickly made her way to Diêm Village. She crossed fields raging with fire, her beautiful clothes torn in the process. As the horrific massacre went on that night, Diệu Nương hid under a heap of corpses in the churchyard. She was rescued the next day, her naked body smeared with blood. The event was so traumatizing that it drove her mad.

Diệu Nương's life wasn't any better after the Communists liberated the village. Her hands were too delicate to raise a hatchet or hoe;

she was too thin-skinned. She had never known hard work in her life, so she was incapable of taking care of herself. Her beauty only alienated her from everyone else. Her singing, during such a desperate time, was meaningless. Poor people were more concerned with survival and having enough to eat.

But at cockcrow each morning and again at sunset, by instinct, she crooned in her sublime voice, mournfully, as though an untamed wind had passed through the bleakest hours of the day. Her songs contained her longing for home, her life as an artist, the spotlight, and her audience. Her youthfulness and beauty had left her the moment she escaped across the front lines and arrived at Diêm Village.

We once had a homeland, a lover...

Many inhabitants of Diêm Village still remember the mournful words of her song. On the evening after the massacre, NVA soldiers were seen parading prisoners through the village, and the captives, shackled in pairs and wearing army fatigues, shuffled with their heads bowed. The soldiers, carrying rifles with bayonets, callously pushed the condemned men forward so that they would quicken their pace past where the villagers lived. On both sides of the road, terrified faces peeked from behind low-hanging doors, searching for relatives among the prisoners, though no villager dared to step outside their homes.

Then, a shadow formed behind a hedgerow beyond the village, and a voice, that of Diệu Nương, began to rise as it usually did at that hour in the day. Her figure emerged from the hedge and followed the condemned men. Her lips trembled, her eyes searching for something familiar to grasp. The prisoners, all male, whose ashen faces looked sunken in the dying light, walked with their backs bent and paid no attention to the apparition. Then an unfamiliar song arose, a voice in mourning. Although the voice was unsteady, the words of the elegy were unmistakable. Diệu Nương continued to sing, hesitantly, through her grief. One of the prisoners joined in with a strong tenor, and soon another followed, until all the condemned men were united in song; her voice was like that of a fleeting kiss across their lips. Now a choir, the soldiers' singing drowned out the misery of their march, but the guards, with their bayonets lowered, did not silence them.

Villagers crowded both sides of the street. They stood solemnly and watched as the captives were marched down the desolate road that cut through the endless plain, until they vanished into columns of dust. Diệu Nương's voice, and the ill-fated prisoners' chorus, echoed behind them into the darkness.

We are brothers at war,
Nothing but worms and ants,
But we once had a homeland, a lover...

•

Now Diệu Nương is dead. Nobody knows where she is buried or the location of the graves of those who were shot with her. Life goes on without memory as it will, as it always has. Time passes, leaves fall down, and the dry seasons as well as the wet appear and fade, year after year.

Eventually, the church at Diêm Village was destroyed by bombs. Weeds now cover its crumbling walls and steps. In the mornings, ravens squawk in its ruins and evoke people's memories of the priest. He has left the village, but nobody knows where he has gone.

On the other side of the river, a field that was once covered by anti-aircraft artillery is now full of eroded, horseshoe-shaped defenses. Here and there are bomb craters, which the passage of time has filled up. The worn path that once connected the artillery field with the village has now become an indistinct white line cutting through thick reed beds along the riverbank.

But the soldiers who were stationed here back then still remember the worn path, the same one on which the cook traveled twice a day to carry food to the battlefield. In the evening, especially at its darkest, the men would stealthily enter the village. When they saw officers or MPs, they would hide in the thick reed beds along this same riverbank and listen for the warbling of quails. The evening mist made their shirts wet.

Back then, soldiers, unless carrying out official duties, were ordered to avoid contact with civilians. The civilians weren't yet educated about the cause for independence, so they were still considered half-*ngụy*. Military regulations were extremely strict, and if someone violated them and unfortunately got caught, they would be severely disciplined. Soldiers, however, still took risks.

The soldiers and the poor civilians engaged in secret affairs, wearing down the path over time. During the day, only the cooks were allowed to travel on the path, but at night it belonged to all who were drawn by sinful desires. Today, each inhabitant of the village still keeps a memento belonging to the soldiers and treasures these reminders of the brave NVA artillerymen. Rumor has it that the secret consorting between soldiers and the villagers created many close relationships, including love affairs, although most were fleeting and without happy outcomes. But love remained love, no matter the reason.

At that time, two male cooks used to transport supplies to the battlefield. Every soldier had wished to become a sous-chef, Cù's assistant. In the company, only Cù was allowed to stay in the village, while his two companions took turns every other month.

I am not sure if the bamboo hut, the storehouse, and the kitchen built right next to the churchyard are still there, but if they are then they must be in ruins. Back then, Cù wanted the parcel of land adjacent to the rector's house, knowing that the location was unlikely to be bombed. The only trouble was having to share the well with the priest, but Cù valued the well because its water was the purest in the village. The priest was young but acted in a dignified way. He was compassionate and more accommodating than the Diêm villagers.

Cù didn't like the villagers because they were unmotivated and pathetic, as they were recent refugees to the area. They subsisted off the bountiful land, but their transformation into farmers had come reluctantly: they did not want to till the land for themselves, living hand to mouth instead, because they had grown dependent on American aid. The villagers were drawn back to the memory of those years, Cù thought, either as soldiers fighting on behalf of the Americans or as the whores who served them. He found them dishonorable, hiding behind their hypocrisy, charlatans without humility, and because they sympathized with the enemy, he thought they must be biding their time for the right opportunity.

The women were the worst. Cù didn't understand why his comrades were so easily fooled by them. The entire company, fifty men total, had survived in the jungle for years without any problems, but when they relocated to the village and closer to its women, troubles began to surface. Unlike Northern women who possessed a strong revolutionary spirit, the women here were not as genuine, hardworking, or responsible. In fact, they were not trustworthy at all. Cù imagined Diêm Village as a cesspool of disease.

"Infected women transmit syphilis and other STDs," Cù warned his subordinates.

Cù was fastidious in selecting apprentices for his cooking team. Many capable men, even if they were quick-witted or humble, were rejected right away. There was one man who looked respectable, but Cù dismissed him back to his unit after only one day in the kitchen, because Cù discovered his true motives.

"If you're a cook, you prepare food like rice and vegetables every day," Cù said, "so your hands must stay clean by not touching anything dirty, especially women."

The villagers were fearful of Cù and nobody was brazen enough to approach the well near his kitchen. If they got along with his assistants and wanted to barter goods or ask questions, they would have to wait until Cù himself went to the battlefield to deliver food.

Twice a day, once in the morning and again in the late afternoon, one of the apprentices would stay behind while Cù and his other assistant distributed cooked meals to the artillerymen. Ních, a mangy but eager Laotian hunting dog, usually led the way. They slogged down Road 14 and turned onto a crooked road that went past the clay-walled and tin-roofed huts of the village, plodding along like hunchbacks. They used their hands to brace the bamboo baskets on their shoulders. The baskets, as large as casks and covered in sackcloth, steamed with the smell of delicious food.

Seeing Ních, the other starving village dogs would run away and hide in the debris without barking. Only poor children, barely clothed, couldn't resist the smell of food and followed the cooks.

"Mister, Mister . . ." they squawked like ravens.

"Hey, little *ngụy*," Cù barked back. "Get lost!"

But if a boy was persistent enough and followed them to the outskirts of the village, Cù would stop and beckon him over, then give the boy some baked manioc, boiled corn, or even a piece of dried fish.

"Here," Cù said, "this is for you. That's all I have. We soldiers eat manioc and wild vegetables, so we don't have much to hand out for free, you know. You should be grateful for our revolution and learn how to farm for yourself to put food on the table. Go tell your mother that. Don't just lazily wait around for food to magically appear in your mouth. The revolution will liberate you, but remember that it won't come easy. Our revolution will take a long time, probably until I die, and probably until you die, too . . ."

(I hear that even now Ních can be seen trotting down the same street. He goes to the riverbank and noses his way around some rusty-green 37mm shells, then jumps into a ditch with an anti-aircraft gun covered in cogon grass. He looks at the rushing river.)

Sometimes, seeing the figures of Cù and one of his two apprentices hauling baskets on their shoulders as they headed down the road with the old, orphaned dog, a village boy would cry out to Cù, "Mr. Cook! Mr. Cook!"

Ních was familiar with this well-traveled path, always going into the village at either dawn or dusk. Nobody dared to pet him. Several villagers who had heard the rumors about Diệu Nương's death believed it was the dog that killed her. Others, who knew even less, were afraid of the dog; they felt a nebulous sense of life's journey coming full circle, one we are condemned to repeat, until we are driven blind and mad.

•

Once, according to the routine, Battery 3 and Battery 4 each sent a soldier to be assistant cook; they would replace Bình of Battery 1 and Tuấn of Battery 2. This situation was unusual, however: Cù let Bình go but kept Tuấn, explaining to the company commander, "Tuấn knows how to do his job well. He might even take over for me."

Tuấn, originally an infantryman, had been severely injured. He could have returned to the North but was talked into voluntarily staying instead. He didn't return to his original unit. In fact, he was transferred to the anti-aircraft battalion. He had been with my company for half a year and became Gunner 3 of Battery 2.

Tuấn was lanky, with yellowing skin and a prominent Adam's apple. He had a formidable scar caused by a bullet, which started at his ear and carved its way to his chin, causing his mouth to look lopsided. Although Tuấn was from Kinh Bắc, he was reluctant to speak and only talked when provoked.[24] Living among boisterous artillerymen, he chose to stay silent—not joining in conversations. He didn't laugh or show any anger. What moral claim was he staking? Tuấn couldn't care less about the Douglas-A1 Skyraiders that swooped low

---

24 A regional stereotype: people from Kinh Bắc tend to be chatty and friendly.

to the ground and dropped bombs, or the mortars that hit defensive forts. His apathy, it seemed, suited his occupation perfectly. As a gunner who shot down Skyraiders on their bombing runs, he was just doing his job. His only responsibility was to remain calm and indifferent while operating the rangefinder that measured the speed and altitude of aircraft.

"Shooting down airplanes gets so dull," Tuấn told me once. "It's not as exciting as being a foot soldier."

"Well," I answered, "it's because you're always assigned to Battery 3. Maybe you can ask the battery commander to switch with me, and join Battery 2."

"I'm just making small talk," he said. "I always follow orders, so I probably shouldn't ask."

"If you hate combat so much, why don't you go back to the North?" Tuấn shrugged his shoulders.

"Is some girl ignoring you?" I went on, "Or did someone just tell you your wife is cheating with a soldier back home?"

"Well," Tuấn replied, twisting his mouth, but said nothing else.

In fact, nobody knew whether Tuấn was a bachelor or not. Even his political advisor knew little about him except for a few details. Tuấn never volunteered information about himself to anyone. Nobody ever caught him writing or reading a letter. He sat quietly at meetings, and barely uttered a response when called on. But Tuấn was gifted at the guitar and, unlike the rest of us, he never had to sway his body or tap his feet to the rhythm when he played. He didn't whistle or hum to keep a tune and strummed mostly to himself. He didn't give a damn who listened.

"What song are you playing, Tuấn?" I asked once, and he simply just grunted in response.

When he became an assistant cook, he took the guitar with him. It was beat-up and covered in scrapes but gave out a marvelous sound. As the story goes, the guitar had been with him since he enlisted, but nobody knew how he was able to carry it around for so many years.

•

Tuấn usually went into the village in the morning, and by afternoon, he and Cù were transporting cooked meals to the battlefield. One day, I saw him carrying on his back a hot pot of soup in a bamboo basket.

"Do you find this job hard, Tuấn?" I asked.

"Yes," he replied.

"What do you think of the women from Diêm Village? Are they like what the other men say?"

"Well . . ."

Tuấn answered my questions without much thought. He was someone who followed orders and rarely showed enthusiasm or contempt. He didn't mind the work and never complained, hardly saying a word, devoting himself instead to the task at hand.

Cù disliked Tuấn at first because Tuấn kept to himself, but Cù eventually got used to it. He didn't consider it a shortcoming. A cook, in fact, had to constantly pay attention and had little time for small talk or airing grievances.

According to the lunar calendar, it was early May, when it often rained at night. The rising waters of the A Rang River flowed into the plain, and the sky overhead roared with thunder. It was on these nights, after a long day of preparing and serving food, that the three cooks had time to themselves. They showered, rested up, and engaged briefly with one another in conversation before lying down in their hammocks. Cù would pull out a bottle of home-brewed alcohol, and each had a glass while listening to Cù give them their work assignments for the following day. During this leisure time, Cù and Bình played cards while Tuấn tuned his guitar and strummed for them. Bình whistled along to Tuấn's music and Cù, dropping his playing cards, would quietly turn around to listen. The men recognized the tune because it was a tune they had heard many times before: *I wander through life without a past. . . .* Outside, the rain fell ferociously, turning the air inside the barracks damp. Yellow light flickered from the oil lamp. A soldier's life, like a sigh, was full of sorrow and boredom.

•

Cù's kitchen and the priest's house faced each other, with a vegetable garden dividing them. They also shared the water well and the same path into the village. The priest's house resembled a cave and had floors and walls that were partially underground. Four earth mounds formed the four corners of the foundation and protected the house from bombardment. The dwelling had no furniture except for a bamboo bed, a straw mat, a wooden pillow, a bookshelf, and an icon depicting saints. Near the door was a ledge where his Catholic parishioners left food for him every morning. Although he would come out several times a day, the priest rarely ventured beyond the churchyard, remaining instead within the church grounds like a hermit.

One day, however, the priest abruptly left the church and vanished from Diêm Village, coinciding with the day Diệu Nương was killed. Baseless rumors swirled about, and many of the stories and much speculation involving her death pointed back to the priest.

•

Like Diệu Nương, the priest had also encountered misfortune. On the day he was ordered by the rector to lead the church in Diêm Village, the Việt Cộng launched an attack. The bus that took him from town to the village had barely come to a stop when it was ambushed from the banks of the A Rang River. A defending T54 tank unexpectedly appeared on Road 14 and was immediately fired on by 130mm cannons. The passengers on the bus panicked and ran; church parishioners, who were gathered outside to welcome the new parish priest, were also terrified and scattered.

As the story goes, on the evening of the Red Fiery Summer campaign when the Americans retaliated by raining bombs on the sea of fleeing people, Diệu Nương was discovered lying alongside the priest. It was the priest who pulled her body, naked and covered in blood, from under a mountain of corpses. He was the one who saved her life and took her under his wing. For several months Diệu Nương lived in the church with the priest, as though she were a nun or female churchwarden.

•

She received many illicit gifts from people which she then handed over to the priest, as though she were a Catholic doing penance for her sins. The gifts included daily food rations taken from the soldiers, or items acquired through plunder. Diệu Nương accepted all the gifts. In return, she took everyone into her bed, sometimes inside her hut located outside the church, at other times on the riverbank or in the grass under the shadowy moon. The men who had slept with her told each other, while drunk, that she was the cause of all kinds of venereal diseases. No one, not even Diệu Nương herself, could remember the first time she gave herself so freely to men. Was it after the Communist liberation of Diêm Village, when her life was completely turned upside-down, that she became so sinful? Or maybe because, as a woman, it is in her nature to sin?

I, along with some others, didn't consider Diệu Nương and her alleged sinful ways despicable or immoral. When we were in each other's company, I was able to enjoy blissful moments that could not have happened elsewhere. After so many years, I still cannot forget, or wish to ever forget, those moments. I envision her walking down a deserted street alone, striding confidently, or sitting in solitude by the river. My heart soars and I become terrified when I think of her now, remembering how I had parted the bamboo mat she used as a door curtain and entered her forbidden bedchamber for the first time.

"Come here, comrade," she had said to me then. "Don't be afraid. There's no one here but me."

I stepped forward and unexpectedly found myself brushing against something warm and velvety, something indescribably buoyant. Instantly, I felt drawn into an unholy temptation.

"Dear comrade, what's your name?" she asked. "Is this your first time with me?"

She was more woman than any woman. Her faultless soul had not been damaged by the cruelties of life since Diêm Village was liberated by the Communists. The way she touched me, our tortured lovemaking, how she kissed and caressed in the throes of passion, her moaning and playful mewing; even after we were left exhausted there still remained in her a kind of feminine and ungodly power.

That night, she held my hand and said, "Are you leaving now? There's still time until the sun comes up. Stay here with me. I have something to tell you . . ."

But no one ever stayed to listen to what she had to say. There was no need to heed her words because we already knew we couldn't grant her the wish she wanted, perhaps because it was too sinful, terrible, and impossible to speak aloud. Maybe Diệu Nương thought there was someone who would fall so madly in love with her that he was willing to take that risk. But in order to keep returning to her bed, no one was foolish enough to say no, so we made promises to her we couldn't keep. All the men who slept with her were like that except one person, the only one who truly kept his word, not just a man giving her empty promises, but someone who would actually go through with it.

•

It was later discovered that Tuấn, as an infantryman, had often visited Diêm Village and had become familiar with Diệu Nương. Our company was not stationed near the A Rang River back then, and she, at the time, was still living inside the church. As the story goes, the inhabitants of Diêm Village were starving when their food supply, given to them by the soldiers after the liberation of the village, ran out. The new revolutionary government that replaced the old American-backed one had ordered everyone to be self-sufficient. Even the Church had to find a way to survive.

Since it was unheard of for a Catholic priest to farm, it was up to Diệu Nương to take care of both herself and the priest. She followed the other village women to clear the land for cultivating manioc, but she had not known the drudgery of work before, so, unable to use a hatchet, she would cry into her open hands instead. The days passed and her plot of land remained unchanged, overgrown wildly with shrubs and trees.

One day, a nearby group of soldiers resting in their hammocks by the river saw her situation. They laughed and ridiculed her at first, the worthless *ngụy* woman—a lazy, good-for-nothing—who was only now experiencing what it meant to do punishing work. But they eventually came around and began to sympathize with her plight— however pathetic—and got off their hammocks, approached her, and offered to help.

From dawn until dusk, the soldiers hacked down trees and cleared the land for Diệu Nương. When it was time to say goodbye, one of the soldiers, namely Tuấn, promised her he would return and help her burn the weeds. Tuấn kept his word and soon the farm became the most fertile in the village. No unwanted tree was left behind. Tuấn and Diệu Nương parted ways but he gave her another promise: he vowed he would return again to plant manioc. Nobody knew how, but Tuấn managed to visit Diệu Nương every five to ten days. He would leave his unit, which was stationed outside town, and cross the countryside to visit her. After the first rain of the season arrived, manioc trees grew in abundance, turning her entire farm plot the color of jade. Tuấn planted gourds around the farm and helped her set up a vegetable garden behind the church.

Around this time, Diệu Nương left the church and moved into a hut Tuấn had built for her outside the village. Because of his commitment, she no longer had that hopeless look about her, which she had had since the day she was rescued in Diêm Village. People now saw her cheerful side and the joy in her eyes. Now and then, Tuấn secretly left his unit to visit her with his guitar, and when they were together, he would play for her while she sang passionately in hushed tones.

I assume they had made a vow. To Tuấn, Diệu Nương had revealed her deepest desire: she wanted to leave this forsaken land behind, in which she found no comfort, and return to that familiar life she knew as a singer before the liberation.

For Tuấn, crossing ten kilometers with checkpoints and minefields was not an impossibility. Those were the peaceful days after the Paris Accords. No aircraft flew overhead, and no cannons fired. Tuấn was madly in love; he wanted peace, so he made his heartfelt vow to Diệu Nương. Not long after that, however, he unexpectedly vanished. Months and years went by without news of him. He did not return to Diêm Village.

Diệu Nương lost her mind and fell back into her sinful ways. She told no one about Tuấn. Although the likeness of him, his words, eventually faded from her mind, her desire to be free carried on without him. The vow they had shared became an unbridled song every morning and afternoon. Each night she sought empty promises from other men, ringing more hollow as the days passed and the war continued. Diêm Village was destroyed by bombs, extinguishing any spark of hope for peace.

•

One rainy evening, while walking with the priest on the road to the church, Diệu Nương heard someone strumming a guitar. As she tiptoed forward and peeked through the underbrush, she saw an oil lamp giving off a ghostly glow. She couldn't see who was playing the guitar, but the melody sounded very familiar and she knew right away it was him. A sort of madness seized her as she slowly made her way to the cooking area. Then, out of nowhere, Ních sprang up from a corner and started barking loudly.

"Who's that?" Cù shouted. He fell out of the hammock clutching his pistol.

Diệu Nương reeled backwards, and when the strumming of the guitar stopped, she turned around and scurried away.

"Stop!" Cù yelled as he reached the door.

A tempest was raging outside. Under the flashes of lightning, the figure of Diệu Nương, soaked and barely on her feet, appeared.

"Ah, it's that whore again!" Cù shouted. "Stop running or I'll kill you!" He chased her outside into the storm, but slipped and fell onto his stomach. As he got to his feet, overcome with fury, he began firing indiscriminately at the moving apparition. Tuấn stopped him by seizing the gun from his hand.

"You fool!" Cù cursed.

Tuấn, letting out a cry, punched Cù in the face without thinking. Then he knocked Cù's gun down onto the muddy ground and chased after Diệu Nương into the storm.

Alarms blared throughout the village. Guerillas from everywhere rushed to the scene.

"When the men come, tell them we have everything under control," Cù told Bình as Bình helped prop him up against the wall. Cù's face, streaked with rain, was covered in blood. Using his shirtsleeve, he swiped at his bloody face and pulled out a broken front tooth. Catching his breath, he told Bình, "Tell them I woke from a nightmare and fired my gun by mistake. . . . Then go look for those two." He sighed. "Why did she have to run away?"

Many years later, when Bình told me about the incident, he said sadly, "If she had not been shot that night, she and Tuấn could have escaped together."

Now, as I look back on the tragedy, I can't understand why Cù acted the way he did. He was the one who had fired the gun at Diệu Nương, but it was also he who, for a long time after that, secretly helped her. The priest would leave his private room open only for Cù, who brought bandages, medicine, and food. The priest refused to see Tuấn.

Cù and Bình revealed nothing. The rest of our company knew nothing about Cù firing his gun and injuring Diệu Nương. Nobody knew about the fight between Cù and Tuấn or the illicit affair between the latter and Diệu Nương. When it came time to rotate out the cook assistants, Cù requested to keep Tuấn.

•

That year, the wet season was unbearably long and dreadful. Finally, I realized what was making me so distraught. I couldn't stop thinking about Diệu Nương. In fact, the whole company looked miserable, as though her absence left us with no reason to stay. There was no news of Diệu Nương, nor was her singing heard again. Her hut was abandoned and fell into ruin. It was overgrown with weeds. Because her body was never found, some believed she had either escaped or died by drowning in the river; others thought she might have been blown apart by a bomb that was dropped directly on her head.

Then, one cloudless day in the dry season, we received news that Diệu Nương was still alive. She had hidden in the church throughout the previous rainy season to recuperate, but before she had fully recovered she escaped again. The priest came out to the artillery field early one morning, under cover of darkness, his cassock wet from the fog, and gave us the news.

"One of your men has taken advantage of her," the priest announced. "The one who doesn't talk with the scarred face. He has betrayed you all, and he's made Diệu Nương betray God." He added that he had informed Cù immediately after he found out about her escape with Tuấn, which happened that same night. Cù, however, chose not to report anything to the company.

Later, as his superior reprimanded him, the bald-headed Cù just stood there and clenched his teeth. "I think we should let them go," Cù said. "But if we want to arrest him, it'll be easy since she's injured and couldn't have gone far. We can use Ních . . ."

I was given the honor of accompanying Cù and the two patrolmen assigned to bring the fugitives back. Ních barreled ahead and led with his nose while Cù held the leash. Armed with automatic rifles, we followed behind the dog. Our orders were to bring Tuấn and Diệu Nương back so that they would not reveal our upcoming troop movements, which were classified. Strangely, Ních did not lead us into town; rather, he led us along the banks of the A Rang River toward the grass-covered floodplains to the west, where we ended at a dense forest.

Dirt filled the crevices of our feet and discouraged us, but we forged ahead. Several hours passed and Ních, diligent as ever, still had their elusive scent. Finally, just as we were about to lose our enthusiasm and turn around, we saw signs of the fugitives. Under a lone *kơ nia* tree shaded by cogon grass, we spotted a colony of ants carrying away rice grains. We saw a cigarette butt nearby. On the flattened grass we noted the unmistakable impression of someone who had been sleeping there.

We were still tailing them as the sun went down and made it to the western side of the grassy floodplains near the mouth of the forest. Feeling exhausted, we stopped by a large creek and sat down to rest. Here, the water erased all clues of where the pair had gone next. The sun was now setting, the afternoon the color of fire, and the silence around us seemed to subsume everything. Then, amid the stillness of the air and the burbling creek, we heard the sound of a strumming guitar carrying through the air like a gentle ripple.

"It's Tuấn's guitar," Cù said softly.

At first we were taken aback, then, listening more closely, we dismissed the sound. We thought it was a trick, but, after regaining our nerves, we heard a gentle voice singing. So we waded across the creek and reached the far shore. A pine forest loomed in front of us, the tall pine trees crowding each other. Wisps of smoke curled up into the air. I stood up and surveyed the scene from a tree trunk. A small campfire with a tin can hanging over it. A hammock strung between a pair of trees. We tried to stay hidden, but a withered branch snapped under our feet and the voice stopped singing. Everything remained at a standstill before I pulled the trigger of my AK rifle and launched a barrage of bullets.

"Comrades," Tuấn said. "We're not here to cause any trouble. Please let us go."

"Shut the hell up!" Bảo, a patrol officer, shouted. "Now raise your hands above your head and come over here."

A moment passed, then several more, but still no response. Cù unleashed Ních and the dog ran forward, barking eagerly toward the underbrush. Just then a bush began to tremble.

"*We are brothers at war . . .*" a voice crooned.

"This is ridiculous!" someone yelled back. "I'll show you brothers at war, sinful woman!"

A sound popped through the air, then others followed. Flashes from our automatic rifles illuminated the black forest. When our bullets finally ran out, everything fell silent. All four of us inched forward and were struck speechless. Behind the foliage hacked down by bullets were the figures of a man and a woman embracing each other, as though the gunfire had joined their bodies that way. Before he closed his eyes and died, it seemed that Tuấn had used his body to shield Diệu Nương from getting shot. Our bullets had gone through both their bodies. Shadows from the campfire fluttered across their naked backs.

We stood there paralyzed. The night grew even more ominous. A terrible weight crushed us, and we felt the responsibility of our actions. The unforgettable smell of gunpowder was all that was left of our madness.

"Hey, Ních, come here," Cù called to the dog. Ních, scared away by the gunfire, had disappeared into the woods.

Crouching over Tuấn and Diệu Nương, I separated their bodies from each other.

•

Two days later, we received new orders to march south. We would never set eyes on Diêm Village again. I regained some measure of equanimity, as did Cù. Whatever future battles lay ahead for us would liberate our tortured souls. We would fight and we would forget. The dry season would burn across the wildlands and turn them the color of honey. Other tempests would come and go, blowing violently the columns of red earth upward; the storms, like angry talons, savagely clawing the ground. This was our last dry season of the war, but we didn't know that then. We had shot to death the messengers of peace, even if peace did finally come.

Copyrights and Permissions

About the Author

Bảo Ninh, the pen name of Hoàng Ấu Phương, was born in 1952 in Nghệ An, a province in central Việt Nam, but has lived most of his life in Hà Nội. He attended Hà Nội University from 1976 to 1981, later graduating from the Nguyễn Du School of Creative Writing in 1986.

At the age of seventeen, Bảo Ninh joined the North Vietnamese Army, where he was among ten soldiers from the 456 in his unit to survive the war. Most of his writing deals with the lingering psychological trauma of war. As Việt Nam's most internationally renowned writer, Bảo Ninh is known primarily for his novel *The Sorrow of War*, which was published in English in 1994. The novel has been translated into several languages and published in around twenty countries, gaining recognition by winning numerous international awards. Although he has won nearly all of Việt Nam's literary prizes and honors, his work is often considered controversial at home because it does not present the war effort as noble and heroic. On the contrary, Bảo Ninh's writing often treats the war as a cause of deep, ongoing psychological suffering. He has been a member of the Việt Nam Writers' Association since 1997.